The Goat, the Wolf,
and the Crab

The Goat, the Wolf, and the Crab

Gillian Martin

Charles Scribner's Sons

NEW YORK

A la Pâquerette

Copyright © 1977 Gillian Martin

Library of Congress Cataloging in Publication Data

Martin, Gillian.
    The goat, the wolf, and the crab.

    I. Title.
PZ4.M381147Go3   [PR6063.A714]   813'.5'4   76-49918
ISBN 0-684-14848-X

1 3 5 7 9 11 13 15 17 19   v|c   20 18 16 14 12 10 8 6 4 2

Printed in the United States of America

Prologue

From *Lettres de mon Moulin*
Alphonse Daudet

Monsieur Seguin never had any luck with his goats.

One after another they ran away up to the mountain, and there the Wolf found them and ate them up.

M. Seguin resolved not to keep a goat anymore.

Then he decided to try one last time and bought himself a little white goat.

She was a little love of a goat, with a silky white coat and dainty hooves and the sweetest nature imaginable. She never pulled at her rope or put her hoof in the bucket when being milked. M. Seguin was ravished.

But one day as he milked her, Blanquette turned her head to him and said, "Listen, M. Seguin. I'm bored here. Let me go."

"What?" cried M. Seguin. "Is your rope too short? I'll lengthen it."

But the goat refused. It would do no good to lengthen the rope. She must go up to the mountain and run free among the wild creatures there, in the fresh air of the high land.

M. Seguin tried every persuasion but the little goat was adamant: it's all very well for cows and asses to be tethered in a field. Goats are different. They need space.

"But the Wolf lives on the mountain," cried M. Seguin. "Why, even my last goat, a particularly brave, strong goat, when she ran away, the Wolf found her and though she fought him all night long till the sun rose, in the morning he killed her and ate her up."

"Poor thing," replied Blanquette. "That's sad. Still, I must go."

M. Seguin grew angry and shouted that he would save her in spite of herself and locked her up in a shed in his field. But he forgot to secure the window and in an instant, Blanquette was away and up the mountain.

She gamboled and played all day in the sunlight, meeting wild creatures who welcomed and admired her, and she was very happy. But as the sun set the air grew chill and in the distance the Wolf howled. Blanquette was afraid and looked down to the valley. There she saw M. Seguin's cottage, tiny like a toy, and the field beside it, and she heard the sad note of M. Seguin's horn, making a last effort to call her home.

Blanquette longed to be safe again and enclosed, but she could not go because she knew that after tasting freedom, any imprisonment would be unbearable.

Then the Wolf came, and little Blanquette saw his huge head and dreadful teeth. She faced him, and resolved that she would fight him as long as M. Seguin's last goat had done, and entered bravely into the battle.

All night long she fought, till her lovely silky white coat was torn and spattered with blood. The night was very long but at last the stars paled and down in the valley a cock crowed. And then little Blanquette laid herself down on the soft grass, and the Wolf fell on her and ate her up.

Everyone knows goats don't kill wolves, not even in fairy tales.

One

He looks as if he's been made up for the part by a TV studio. His hands are too clean. He wears his watch too far down his wrist. His hair is unnervingly luxuriant for a man his age, and the parting too perfect. Perhaps he does shampoo ads on the side. Or maybe it's a wig. Very expensive.

Hannah smooths the wrinkles out of her kid gloves and stretches the fingers one by one while she waits for him to speak. Go on, she silently bids him. Say it, then you can have your money and I can go home.

He leans forward on the far side of the desk, clasps his hands, and regards them long and fixedly. Then he looks up at her.

Oh, she admires, still silent. So sincere. He *must* do ads on the side. Her mouth quirks up at the corners, and he clears his throat at once and embarks on his sincere talk.

"Mrs. Jackson. I have the results of your tests, and, uh . . ."

Hannah stops listening. She has already decided. She thinks instead of how she will have her hair restyled later after lunch. Lunch will be lovely. She is going to have smoked salmon with a little brown bread and no butter. Then a beautiful salad, followed as a treat by patisserie. And two glasses of wine, dry and white and very cold. Then hair—and a manicure? Maybe.

He's still talking, his voice rising and falling creamily. Hannah focuses on him again and decides she doesn't want to sit here any longer, so she interrupts without warning.

"I have made up my mind already what I'm going to do," she says. "Before I came here, I knew what you were going to tell me, and I've had time to think about it." He is disconcerted. He clears his throat again and adjusts his sincere posture. "I repeat, Mrs. Jackson, the percentage of complete cures is very high. In two or three years' time, you'll look back on this as a rather bad dream."

"On the contrary, Doctor. In two or three years' time, I shan't look back at all."

She observes irritation, annoyance, creep into his expression, quickly subdued by years of experience with sick, shocked women. Professional sympathy wins, and he smiles a small, encouraging smile.

"I'll arrange the operation at once. You can be in the hospital in a very few days, and it will all be over before you know it."

"No," she says.

"Some family problem? Surely this is more important? Surely you can arrange . . ."

"No."

"I'm afraid I don't understand."

"Clearly. You *don't* understand. I have decided, as I told you, what to do."

"Yes?"

"Nothing."

Silence. He is confused now. He leans back in his chair and some of the gloss seems to go off his hair.

"You don't mind if I smoke, do you," Hannah states, taking cigarettes from her bag and lighting one. His mouth opens, then closes. What can he say.

"Mrs. Jackson," he begins again. "Have you understood what I've been telling you?"

"I wasn't listening," Hannah says through a smoke ring. "But had I been, I'm quite sure I would have understood.

After all," she continues with relish, "in my own way, I expect I'm as clever as you are."

This is a discovery she has made during the week since she last saw the doctor. She has been provoked into thought after years of avoiding it, first consciously, then by habit. She is persuaded that she has seriously underestimated herself, accepting as fact the opinion of mother and husband that she hadn't the stature to be a free-acting person. Thinking, she has discovered that she disagrees with them, not only on this point but on others too, and that her own conclusions are as valid as anyone else's. She blames them for the lost sense of her own worth and for the squandered years, and herself almost equally for not rejecting the benevolent tyranny.

The doctor takes off his glasses and rubs his eyes. This woman is too difficult for a man his age, too much of whose energy is expended in supporting the suffering while keeping up with his wife's social ambitions and looking after his hair. And he feels his bowels shift and worries briefly that the feeling is about to be translated into bubbling sound.

"Let's have some coffee," he says wearily.

"All right, if you like."

They sit silently as they wait for the coffee. Hannah smokes luxuriantly, blowing a cloud of smoke at the disapproval of the nurse who brings the coffee in. He looks into space when the nurse has gone out.

"Let me explain."

"No. Let me." Hannah takes pity on him. "I suppose I owe you an explanation. You have been telling me the tests are positive. That I have cancer and that I will die without an operation."

He nods.

"And I," Hannah continues clearly, "have been telling you that I have decided not to have an operation."

"But that inevitably means . . . look, it's curable. It's very early on. We can excise it completely. Almost guarantee you a total recovery."

"My mind is quite made up."

"Oh for God's sake," he snaps impatiently, crossly, raising his voice. Hannah smiles.

"That's better." She nods approvingly. "It exasperates me when you're so bland. It suggests that I'm so anonymous that I produce no reaction in you."

"You are not anonymous, Mrs. Jackson," he assures her with feeling. "But, forgive me, you are being astoundingly foolish. It's a shock, I know, and shock causes odd reactions. Look, I'll talk to your husband today, and then see you both together . . ."

"No. It's not a shock. I told you, I've had time to think about it and I've made the decision. And I wish you not to talk to my husband."

"This is insane. Insanely selfish." Agitated, he tries to rile her.

"Oh yes. Supremely selfish. It's the first autonomous decision of my life and the only one that is entirely selfish. I am thinking purely of myself."

"But it would cause tremendous pain to your family. And difficulties. And you yourself . . . have you really thought about it? You feel well enough now. But you won't. You will feel less and less well, until you are in pain. The pain will get intense. You will need nursing, attention, help. The pain will worsen. Finally you will die."

He sits back, waiting for his sternness to produce results.

"I know," Hannah says. "I've looked it up. I know all that. Had you the time and patience, I would try and explain my reasons."

"Try," he commands.

She regards him speculatively. Is it worth her while to try? Could he, a man who can influence events, understand the reasoning of a woman who has never done that? And now, at the end, has an opportunity? Could he acknowledge the charm of not considering how a thing will affect any number of other people and of just going on one's selfish way rejoicing? Perhaps.

"I am forty-two years old," she begins. "My children are grown up. My husband is well employed. I have a marriage

4

and a style of life that millions would envy. I have had my teeth looked at twice a year. I have had my eyes tested at suitable intervals, and, as you know, I have had cervical smears taken as recommended. I have done my washing on Mondays, cleaned out my cupboards regularly, and lain dutifully on my back and thought of England. I have kept my figure reasonably well and paid passing attention to changes in fashion. I have done everything as and when it was expected of me, and in the doing I have abdicated my self entirely.

"I have lived my life without passion. I have never lain down on the pavement outside the American Embassy. I have never thrown pepper at foxhounds or boycotted South African oranges. In fact, I have not done anything at all without someone else's interests being the prime factor. This is the last opportunity. I insist on doing this in my own way."

Silence. He twists a pen between his fingers, purses his lips, thinks. He is a busy man. He has troubles of his own. Why doesn't she help him?

She goes on. "I have been thinking, these last days, of the indignity of being a woman of my age who has never been responsible for her actions. First my parents, then my husband. Always someone who, with the best motives, regulated my life. Lived it for me, almost. And I, in my ignorance, gave my life up to them and had no control over it. It has to stop."

"But you don't have to *die,* for God's sake, just to prove a point. You decide to have the operation. That's a decision too. Make it now."

"No. It would negate the value of having already made one if I were to retract at the first dispute."

"Oh, pride. Pride. How can you let stupid pride condemn you? Cutting off your very life to spite yourself."

"You're wrong. Pride is very important. I've been proud of my children and my husband and all sorts of things. But never of me. I'm not now, but I have made a reasoned decision and I shall stand by it. A *reasoned* decision. And you still don't see. I believe in natural selection. All those zoo people, for instance. They make me cross. Tigers, crocodiles, 'threatened species.' Might it not be that their part in evolution is finished and it's just meddlesome to try and change the order of things? All right, perhaps they do become extinct because man hunts them or ruins their habitat, but may that not be the way the overall plan was meant to work? I don't want to go on living forever anyway. A hundred years ago, I'd have had no option. I'd rather let this take its course naturally. And think how you would be preaching acceptance to me yourself if this were some long, wasting nonkiller."

"You wouldn't treat a child with leukemia?"

"Of course. I'd try anything. My wilder emotions would be involved. But my instinct would still tell me to stop beating my head against God."

"God. How can you believe in God, talking the way you do?"

"Very easily. But because He is God, I don't expect to understand Him. I have simply decided to have my way in this."

"I must speak to your husband."

"I can't stop you. But it will make no difference."

He doesn't believe that. He is angry. He is worried. He feels menaced. All this and moss in his lawn too.

"There's no more to be said," Hannah says. She rises and holds out her hand.

"Don't feel bad. You've done all you ought to do, or want to do."

She leaves him standing behind his desk wondering whether he has been seeing a rather irritating manifestation of shock, or whether she really believes and means what she says. He thinks she does, at least for the moment.

She leaves the hospital and emerges into a cold March air. The wind is keen, blowing dust and scraps of paper along the gutters, pinching people's faces so that they walk with their heads down or turned to one side.

Hannah stands on the steps and looks around. Everything looks very interesting, invested with glamour almost. And herself is the most interesting of all. She feels childlike. She is not unhappy. She is released from the threat of old age, from senility, loneliness, incontinence. Everything has been simplified for her, brought to its ultimate simplicity. All she has to do is live the rest of her life—and do it free at last from the malaise of the spirit that has undermined her for years. There is no need any longer to pretend this, concede that. Ideally, she acknowledges, she should have lived all her adult life this way, but she has been protected and spoiled and cheated out of it. She doesn't want to start afresh armed with this new adulthood. She's a little afraid that she mightn't manage to do it right even the second time around. Better to achieve the dignity of doing one thing with grace and then to bow out, leaving a clear-cut memory of herself alive, rather than to evaporate slowly and boringly.

Lunch, she thinks, and turns toward the Underground. Then she changes her mind and hails a taxi instead.

Two

Time has started to pass and Hannah is keenly aware of it. No more of the blurred edges the past years had. Everything has a clarity and an importance that delight her. Everything interests her enormously.

She has told her husband nothing yet. She assumes, correctly, that the doctor will allow a day or two to elapse before he speaks to him. Not long, because time is important, like with abortions, she thinks. They want to remove the crab before it gets big enough to fight back. She will tell Henry herself very soon. He hasn't noticed any change in her. He doesn't notice her very much at all because they have been married for twenty years and she is a habit, like his pipe, noticed only when absent. When he talks to her, he hardly ever looks at her, and if he does, she wonders what he sees. Because, to be fair, she admits that for years she has encouraged his apartness. Since, in fact, the time when she realized she didn't love him but was completely dependent on him. It seemed the only course. He seemed happy enough and she wasn't actively unhappy, and there were marriage vows and the children; one might as well jog along with as little aggravation and as much good temper as possible.

Now, at the beginning of the rest of her life, she sees this as a shameful mistake. A groveling cowardice. Poor Henry. He deserved better. Not his fault or hers that they don't love each other. He says from time to time that he loves her, and she believes that he believes it to be true. But she believes also that what he loves is an idea of her, not her as she is or was or ever could be.

So here is Hannah, lying in the bath, thinking about Henry, because tonight she must tell Henry and he won't like it. She feels she ought to care more that Henry won't like it but she can't. Telling Henry something he didn't like has always till now made her nervous. There must be a numbness somewhere from a little grain of shock. Interesting.

Henry. There is evidence of him all over the bathroom, which she hasn't yet cleaned today. A smear of toothpaste on the mirror. A razor lying in the washbasin. A dust of beard around the rim. The linen box with underpants trailing from under its lid like pearls from a treasure chest.

He's an awfully nice man, Henry, though messy. She would love him if she could. It would be convenient for a start, and he deserves loving, but she has tried and tried and keeps coming to a halt at liking. This is nothing to be ashamed of because it is not a thing she can help, and she has done her best to make him comfortable. Twenty years ago, she believed she loved him passionately and forever. She laughs, thinking back to the certainty she had felt, firmly based on a complete lack of evidence or experience. And Henry too, too ignorant to know how little he knew. She thinks back over the steps that brought them together.

Hannah's mother brought her daughter up carefully. She was a woman who meant well, guessed at a world beyond her experience, wanted it for her child, and feared it too much to let her go in search of it. Her ideal was an assured income, an inside lavatory, and a reliable husband with negative virtues, who didn't drink to excess, didn't beat his wife, didn't "bother" her. Who could want more? Except, of course, an obedient child who didn't confuse her with desires she couldn't comprehend or friendships she didn't approve and who didn't leave fingermarks on the furniture.

Life was a jungle where Woman crept timorously through the undergrowth, stalked eternally by the twin predators, Man and Poverty. To escape the one, she had to settle for the other, sooner or later. Of the two, Man was the lesser evil, if he didn't drink to excess, etc., etc.

"Security," she used to say. "That's what you must aim for. Just a bit of security." And security meant money in the bank.

"Take care of the pennies and the pounds will take care of themselves," she preached, laboriously adding savings certificate to savings certificate, never venturing into the mine fields of shares or bonds, which were the province of men because they knew about these things by nature. Except for Hannah's father.

She might have been a beautiful woman, had she realized it was allowed. Beauty was not for the ordinary woman in search of security. Film stars might be beautiful, but look at the way they lived, divorced every five minutes, painting their nails, smoking and drinking. All part and parcel. No, the ordinary woman who washed her face with soap and water and settled for the appearance God gave her, kept a clean house and obedient children, was by definition a good woman and deserved security.

Hannah, at the age of ten, was given a little book to read. It told about little seeds, smaller than a pinhead, performing a complicated game of Box and Cox in ladies' insides. Then mysteriously one little lady seed met a gentleman seed in a tunnel, they united coyly and without further explanation became a baby.

"Where did the gentleman seed come from?" Hannah asked, having read and not understood.

"From the father," her mother answered shortly. She was ironing spiritedly, the kitchen filled with a damp, warm scorch smell. Bang bang, went the iron, slapping down fiercely on a starched sheet. So much passion to iron a sheet.

"But how?" Hannah persisted. "If the tunnel is inside the lady, how can the gentleman seed get in?"

In her mind's eye, she saw a gentleman in a bowler hat, carrying a briefcase, walking along the High Street. He sees a lady coming toward him and accosts her, leaning forward and raising his hat. "Good morning, Madam. Would you like one of my seeds?" He offers her one. "Thank you very much," she says, popping it into her mouth. "That was lovely."

"Is that why you tell me not to take sweets from strangers? Because I'd have a baby?"

"Tch tch." Mrs. Owen frowned, ironing faster than ever. "No no no." She brought the words into her mouth but found they would go no farther. They refused to leave her lips until by an effort of will, a painful performance of what she saw as, maternal duty, she spat out, "They have Sexual Intercourse."

"What's that?"

"Oh my lord," said Mrs. Owen with strangled anguish, "stop pestering me. I gave you that book to tell you all about it—and to warn you."

She slammed down the iron and gathered up the pile of folded washing and stomped out of the kitchen. Hannah, left wondering, was confused even further by a parting shot from halfway up the stairs.

"And don't you ever say you've got a backache if there's a man about. Or a boy." There rested the whole of Hannah's instruction on the facts of life and love and marriage.

When Hannah was seventeen she went with a school party to France. It was the first time she had stayed away from her mother and she was crushed before the departure by advice from her.

"Mind you don't get fleas. French people are very dirty. Don't sit on any lavatory seats. Mind you don't leave Miss Edwards's side for a moment, and if you do get lost, find a kind-looking woman, not one of those painted ones, and tell her. Don't trust any man, especially if he seems anxious to help. They're the worst sort," said Mrs. Owen, who had once visited London on a day trip.

"Oh, Mother," Hannah wailed, trying not to listen but knowing from experience that the words were dripping into her subconscious mind and would be likely to spoil everything.

"Hannah, you're young. You don't know the world. It's full of dangers for a well-brought-up girl."

"But you've never been to France. How do you know?"

"I know what I know." Mrs. Owen nodded sagely, knowing nothing.

Hannah and her friend Susie stood looking into a shop window on the Rue de Rivoli. It was a day marked "free shopping" on their itinerary. They were looking at underwear the like of which they had never imagined, satin knickers, slippery and trimmed with lace, bras that might have been functional but didn't look it and weren't meant to.

"Gosh, look at that nightie," Susie breathed, making a damp patch on the glass. "It's like a party dress almost. D'you suppose people wear things like that, really?"

"They do in the films."

"Yes, but that's not real, is it?"

"I expect people must buy them, otherwise they wouldn't sell them."

"My mother told me she had a black nightie for the night of her wedding. She said Dad said it looked pretty hanging on the end of the bed."

Hannah flushed an uncomfortable red.

"Does your mother talk to you about things like that?"

"Now and then, when she's in the mood. Doesn't yours?"

"Never. I don't know how I ever came to be born."

The sudden eruption of such a gross confidence left Hannah ashamed and fearful.

"My mother says you have to know these things, about boys and so on, I mean, for your own protection," Susie said, gratified that she was better informed.

"I know about boys," Hannah retorted dishonestly. "I've read about it all, I mean."

The conversation faltered, neither able to add to what had been said. Then Susie pointed.

"Look at those knickers there. The legs aren't joined together. How funny. I suppose it's to make it easier when you use those awful French lavatories."

Hannah studied the knickers.

"They're funny, the French," she mused. "They're not a bit shy about lavatories are they? Remember that man in the public convenience? I nearly died."

Overcome by secret visions of what his occupied hand had been holding, they both bent to examine the knickers again.

"I don't know though," Susie mused, then blushed violently. "Oh gosh. I've just thought. Oh, it couldn't be . . ."

"What?" Hannah asked, unsuspecting. "What couldn't it be? I don't understand."

Seventeen and still a child. Grown-up Hannah smiles to herself in the bath, looking down the length of her body and mildly congratulating herself. It's not a bad body for forty-two. Quite firm and, apart from a few stretch marks, unblemished. The legs are slender, and she has long since come to terms with the smallness of her bust. Even at seventeen it wasn't that her bust was small that anguished her as much as that the spare roll of flesh below it was bigger. If the bust were bigger, she thought, it might overhang the fat and make it seem less noticeable. But at seventeen you're supposed to be so happy, so expectant, so sure that the world is a wonderful present just waiting for you to unwrap it. That's not the way of it at all. It's gift-wrapped, all right, but more the way a parcel bomb might be deceptively pretty. You know somewhere inside you, when you're seventeen, that when you untie the ribbon, the world is quite likely to go off bang in your face. You know there must be a safe way to unwrap it but all you can do is be very wary and hope for the best, while thousands look on, ready to choke with laughter when you do it wrong.

So sad, Hannah thinks, looking at her long legs in the bath, that she never came any closer to the divided-satin-knicker circuit. She would have been a different person if she had.

Hannah and Susie in the Rue de Rivoli then, heads together, hating their youth and round sweet faces and plump bodies, too young to know they looked toothsome and delicious. A hand touched Hannah's shoulder and the girls snapped around to see a tall heavy man, big-nosed, sandy-haired, standing behind them.

"Pardon," he said in English. "I can help you? I overhear you don't understand something."

Hannah dropped her handbag and Susie began to giggle

mirthlessly. Hannah was annoyed with her. She bent to shovel her handbag together and stood up again.

"Thank you," she said coldly, prickingly aware that she was talking to a Strange Man, "it's perfectly all right."

She turned sternly away with a muttered "Come on" to Susie.

The man looked stricken.

"I am sorry," he said, falling into step beside them, his voice deep, pulsating with emotion. Distress was written all over him. "You think I . . . forgive me. I assure you I am engineer and very correct."

The girls were now both out of their depth. Neither mother had covered this adequately. He looked like someone's kind uncle, probably rich. He was clearly upset that they had mistaken him for the sort of Strange Man who might offer sweets to little girls. And there were, after all, two of them. Safety in numbers was another maternal axiom. They hovered, fidgeting with their handbags, waiting for a ghostly mother to appear from somewhere and tell them what to do next.

"My name is Armand Fouchet." The man bowed. "You see, I am not dangerous at all. It was simply that I heard you say you did not understand and as I speak English, though so badly, I thought I might translate."

"Oh no." Both girls hurried to keep him away from the knickers.

"Will you allow me to offer you a drink at that café, to show that you forgive me? What harm? An old man like me and two beautiful young ladies? Please?"

"All right," Susie suddenly agreed. Hannah stared at her. "It's all right," Susie hissed while Armand Fouchet looked studiously the other way. "I've got my penknife if he turns funny. Come on. It's a lark."

They went with him the few yards to a pavement café where they sat and listened while he talked. About England, about the Louvre, about the shops, and all the time Hannah's mind ticking.

She shifted minutely in her chair as she felt his fingers

14

touch her knee. It must be accidental. His hand was warm. Her plump knee enjoyed the sensation even while she, with a fixed silly smile, pretended not to notice and a most unfamiliar pins and needles ran up and down her back. Her eyes glazed and the silly smile froze as the hand, with unmistakable deliberation, crept up her thigh. What should she do? Mother had not covered this either. The hand, like a warm, nuzzling little animal, crept higher. Armand Fouchet was leaning innocently toward the girls, both hands out of sight beneath the table, outwardly doing no more than talking equally to each girl.

Hannah tried to signal to Susie, but Susie had a distracted air and was looking into the middle distance. The hand by now was decidedly off limits and seemed to have grown extra fingers too.

Desperate, crimson, appalled, Hannah knew something had to happen. The exploring fingers were toying with the edge of her sensible interlock knickers . . . the shame of being caught wearing sensible knickers . . . another instant and it would be in the forbidden continent, the place that Hannah's grandmother had once jollily called "the shop," for which Hannah's mother had never forgiven her. Frantically she tipped her handbag onto the ground and, mumbling incoherently, dropped to her knees under the table to retrieve it and hide her fiery face. There she knelt, weak with shock at the sight of Armand Fouchet's heavy tweedy knees and Susie's spread thighs, bulging slightly over her stocking tops, with a ginger-haired hand snugly tucked in above.

Hannah hasn't remembered that for years. She laughs now with sympathy for young Hannah. Perhaps it would have been a very good thing if Armand Fouchet had caused the world to go bang in her face. The explosion might have blown her into some sort of shape and saved her from simply growing older and becoming an amorphous blob, human frogspawn. She tries hard to recall what happened next but it's gone, evaporated into time, and she is left transfixed forever on her hands and knees under a café table, unaware that the iniquitous interlock knickers, roundly exposed among chair and table legs, are lifting a few Parisian hearts and sending smiles gusting along the Rue de Rivoli.

Back from Paris, Hannah believed she was a woman of the world. She had had an Experience. Her mother was disturbed by the unexplained change she noted.

"It's a good thing you're leaving school. That Miss Edwards is a bad influence. All this going abroad. It unsettles a well-brought-up girl."

That was true. Hannah was unsettled. Thoughts troubled and excited her as they never had before. The remark she had so easily made to Susie now weighed heavily. How had she come to be born? Surely her mother and father had never? Her mother, vested, brassiered, corseted, knickered, petticoated, a daunting prospect surely, and her little father, so easily daunted, so small and monochrome. Perhaps there was another way for the sensible woman in search of security? And could she really accept her mother's claim that men were all alike, dangerous predators, when her father's timid presence denied it absolutely? Poor little Mr. Owen. If woman was truly the archetypal victim, how did it come about that Mrs. Owen, and other mothers known to Hannah, were so powerful? They ruled their households, scolded their husbands, decided and demanded standards of behavior from them and their children, were the arbiters of everything.

Hannah has still not resolved that question. The elements of that kind of matriarchal dominance must have been left out of her character. She shelves the question once again, adds more hot water to her bath, and settles back again comfortably.

By the age of eighteen, Hannah, while loving her parents, had come to dislike her mother and feel an impatient pity for her father. He, pale, powerless provider of security, thereupon achieved the glory that had eluded him all his life by dying quietly of a very undramatic but conclusive heart attack.

Oh what splendor then for Mrs. Owen. Born to be a widow, she triumphed, supported by the insurance money. Mr. Owen, in the telling of him, grew to be a big, beautiful man, devoted to the worship of Mrs. Owen and highly successful in the world of affairs. Safely dead, he no longer needed clean underpants, ironed shirts, or his marital rights. Nor did he leave dirty footmarks on the scrubbed floor. What a pity, Hannah thought, that he couldn't have been dead while he was alive. He would have been twice the man and would have liked it much better.

Alas for Hannah. With her father nicely settled in Valhalla, all her mother's power was now directed at her. Hannah must be groomed for her future role as Unmarried Daughter and saved from servitude to a Man. With a little luck, Mrs. Owen intended to live forever, to continue her search for security, and a handmaiden was needed. To be fair, she loved Hannah but could not accommodate the thought that Hannah was capable of, or could want, an existence separate from her own. Whenever any project was suggested, Mrs. Owen would very slowly arrive at her inevitable decision, saying as she communicated it, "You've had no experience, Hannah. You must be guided by me."

"How am I ever to get any experience?" Hannah would rail impotently.

"Just be thankful you have a mother who cares," Mrs. Owen would sigh. "With the little bit I've managed to put away by sacrificing all my life, we'll be all right as long as we're careful."

Hannah was suffocated by being all right as long as she was careful. She knew she must get away. But how? How did a young girl with no experience and a widowed mother leave home?

Hannah lay awake nights, raging silently. During the long, exhausting, empty days she did her share in the house and escaped into daydreams, and made pots of tea for Mrs. Owen's afternoon callers, smiling glassily while she served it and thinking murderous thoughts.

"She's a good girl. A real comfort," Mrs. Owen agreed indulgently with her widowed visitors, and Hannah smiled on and worked out bloody schemes to destroy them all.

Into this sorry picture came Henry. Henry was good to his

mother within limits. He visited her often and gave her little treats, but he didn't live with her. He was often cheeky and teased her, making her go pink and display a set of dimples that she had used thirty years earlier with the effect of heavy mortar fire on the departed Mr. Jackson senior. When Henry drove his mother to visit Mrs. Owen one afternoon, he was as delighted to see Hannah as Hannah was to see him.

Henry lived in London. Such glamour. Henry was a dentist. Such security. Henry was twenty-eight. Such a good age. Henry was single. Such luck. Henry was in Mrs. Owen's good books. Such an irresistible range of virtues. Hannah fell in love. He was quite good-looking too, and he had a car and some money. Hannah didn't know that he sulked if he didn't get his own way, or that he shared his mother's prejudiced view of himself, or that he solved arguments by shouting more loudly than his opposition. But he was a well-meaning man and thought Hannah sweet and shy and pretty, well brought up, and in every way qualified to be fallen in love with. Henry fell in love.

The two mothers recognized their luck. The ideal would have been for Henry and Hannah to remain unattached to anyone and so be able to concentrate their attention on their mothers. But ideals are not often achieved, so this was a good second best. So blessings were given and apart from disputes about the actual ceremony, all went smoothly and Hannah found herself, in an astonishingly short time, a married lady in London. The mystery of sex was disappointingly though vigorously demonstrated to and on her, and she was happy, borne along on a wave of euphoria. Life was going to happen to her at last.

Playing house was a lovely game for a little while until it stopped being the big match and slipped into being a daily training session. Then Hannah saw that she was playing Henry's house and that she was Henry's wife. No one spoke of Hannah's house, or Hannah's husband. Hardly ever did anyone say Henry and Hannah. It was Henry and his wife or, increasingly, just Henry. Because Henry told everyone, including Hannah, that she was a real little homebody who didn't care for society, who cared only for her home. Hannah, reacting as when she was told by her mother that she really did like rice pudding and it was good for her and anyway mother knew best, swallowed it like the rice pudding and hoped it was good for her.

Among Henry's friends a reputation grew over Hannah, like moss over a stone, for never complaining or arguing or making herself noticeable. When the telephone rudely interrupted important masculine talk at Henry's club bar, it was never Henry's wife furiously shrilling at the other end. None of his friends could quite remember her name at the first try, nor her face. Henry congratulated himself and graciously accepted his friends' congratulations on having such a satisfactory marriage, not noticing that they really didn't envy him much.

The truth was that Hannah was a bit afraid of Henry. He had such a loud voice. If she tentatively mentioned a spoiled meal or a lonely evening, it was always in an apologetic way so that she could quickly retreat into not having meant to complain and of course she realized how hard he worked and how lucky she was.

She began to dream dreams and cast timidly calculating looks at men in the streets.

And then she found she was pregnant.

Three

Hannah rouses herself and gets out of the bath. She feels a trace of guilt at spending so long there in the morning when good women should be at their housework. The bath has been her refuge. She has spent a measurable percentage of her life in it. The bathroom has a lock on the door, there are creams and oils and scented potions. Steam blurs the mirror and makes her mistily reflected face beautiful, eliminating faults and blemishes, making her eyes big and dark with distended pupils. She has dreamed dreams in bathrooms all her life it seems. She has been a mysterious Cinderella at a thousand balls, ridden off into the desert on a hundred milk-white horses, been raped by racing drivers, told Henry precisely where his faults lie. The dialogues are always satisfactory in the end because she supplies both sides, and if it doesn't come right, she can go back and start again.

Now she decides briskly to tell Henry this evening. She wishes she didn't have to tell him at all, but if she doesn't the doctor will. She hopes she can make him see it sensibly, because that will make it more comfortable for them both. She sees no reason to tell her sons yet, if ever. They are grown-up now and don't belong to her anymore. She doesn't belong to them either.

They belonged to her when they were babies, but it's almost impossible to relate two grown men with beards and hairy chests and mighty thighs to the bald, dimpled boy-babies whose toes and bottoms she kissed and crooned over. They lived in a charmed circle, she and they, when they were tiny. They had a country all their own, with its own language and customs, and when they made forays into the world outside it was as adventurers, interested but wary, and they were always glad to scurry back to their secret places. She was vital then. The boys could not survive without her, and when she was with them, she used to feel quite real.

Henry said she was bringing them up to be pansies because she never let them fight. She always nipped fights in the bud by finding some irresistible distraction. Henry said they should fight if they wanted to, but it was easy for her to over-ride him because he wasn't there at the right moments. She took a little pleasure in having this small supremacy over him. The unadmitted separateness was becoming established.

Poor Henry. On reflection, she sees that his petulance then was understandable and that she dealt thoughtlessly with it. She dealt with him the way he had habitually dealt with her, denying him involvement in her being, a female retaliation to her exclusion from the real world. Consciously? Honestly, yes, in part. A tit-for-tat retaliation. See how you like being the one who stands on the sidelines, never allowed to play, but not allowed to go away? For a spell, she had been content to be absorbed with and by her babies and Henry had got nothing but crumbs, if anything. "Crumbs" remind her of Henry, formal and stern in stiff white collar, his dignity impaired by pearl barley spilled on the kitchen floor that made him roller-skate as he walked, holding up a crustless loaf and demanding to know why all the crust had been trimmed off.

"The boys have eaten it. I told them it would make their hair curl," she said cheerfully.

"I have had no crust. I like crust. My mother always cut the crusts off especially for me. With butter."

"Well, their mother cut the crusts off for them. With butter and jam," she retorted meanly and deliberately, not seeing little-boy Henry puzzled and upset behind the dark suit and stiff collar.

"You are spoiling those children," Henry began, meaning, "You are neglecting me," but she had cut off the argument, strong then in her mother-power.

"You teach them to fight then. You hit them and tell them there's no Father Christmas, and they can't have crusts with jam. Crusts are good for their teeth anyway. You said so."

"Jam is bad for their teeth," Henry had shouted, storming out.

Oh dear, she thinks now, putting on lots of eye shadow. Poor Henry. I was doing it to him because he did it to me.

She had always had an understanding, whether she admitted it or not, that her time with the boys was only to last as long as they were dependent on her. Only alone with the boys did she feel that power, that spark of living, but babies grow inexorably. Outside, anonymity dogged her as much as ever. Old ladies would coo at the children, tossing odd remarks at her but never looking or listening. The doctor would prod and examine one or the other of them and call her "Mother" in a distracted tone, hurrying her along impatiently if she paused to think before answering a question.

"Have they had chicken pox, Mother?"

"Well . . ."

"Yes or no? Chicken pox, Mother."

Once Hannah tried to rebel.

"Look," she said, hearing her voice strange and plaintive, "I'm here, you know. Inside this coat. I live and breathe. I am here."

The doctor gave a jolly impatient professional chuckle.

"Come along now, Mother. Better have an evening out at bingo, eh?" he answered, and Hannah dispassionately watched him write "N.B. Mother neurotic" on her children's card and knew her rebellion had achieved nothing but damage.

But she hadn't minded unbearably. The children knew she was there inside her coat. They even loved her coat when she wasn't in it and would run to it where it hung in the hall and cuddle closely into it because it breathed of her.

It was at this time, when the house was filled with the milky warmth of small children, and Hannah, saturated with motherhood, had any number of reasons for not being a wife, let alone a mistress, that Henry came to the conclusion that he must find himself a serious interest and started the research for his major book.

He had failed in his attempts to keep Hannah's concentration on himself. He was bruised by and jealous of her relationship with the boys. He loved the boys dearly and wanted to be a hero to them, but he didn't know their language, and circumstances excluded him from wide areas of their little lives. He hoped for better things as they grew and went to school and Hannah's excuses lost their power. And his turn had come, as the boys grew perceptibly away from her, knowing she was so securely theirs that they didn't have to worry about noticing her, and Henry became increasingly glamorous as the source of pocket money and stories of sporting prowess that he was never called upon to prove. But Hannah never came back to Henry. She was always there, available, consenting, but consenting is not the same thing as being eager. Not at all. And he was very eager.

So, doggedly drilling teeth and filling cavities, Henry with his white coat and very clean hands fought against fantasy in his consulting room. He began to see his drill as an erotic instrument. Wild pictures careered through his mind of the uses he might put it to, and sometimes his face would turn red and the tips of his ears white and poor Henry would have to maneuver awkwardly from behind his patient in order to hide the agitation manifest under the starched white coat. This, thought Henry, was bad. Not only might it get out of control, causing unimaginable trouble, but it didn't satisfy him at all. It didn't fit into the jigsaw puzzle he was working on that, when finished, would represent a Complete Man. A good citizen who worked conscientiously during working hours, washed his car on Sundays, didn't annoy his neighbors with garden bonfires, and voted Tory. A man who was good to his mother, within limits, couldn't let himself fall prey to dreams of hurling himself onto the laps of captive lady patients whose mouths were clamped with ironmongery so that they couldn't scream for help as he did dreadful things to them with a dentist's drill.

The obvious solution was to do dreadful things, naturally not with a dentist's drill, to his wife, but Hannah had no interest in dreadful things it seemed. She too had dreams, but in them she was partnered by a faceless, nameless man, and all she knew about him was that he wasn't Henry. Henry excited was absurd. He put a great deal into his side of conjugal relations—Hannah found she couldn't think of them as lovemaking—heaving and panting and sweating, and Hannah had stopped minding long ago that he gave no indication that he noticed she was there, she Hannah, beyond her obviously necessary physical presence. Henry would relieve himself and Hannah would wait for it to be over so that she could console herself with dreams until she fell asleep. The dreams were of necessity inexplicit because she had no experience to draw on and relied on what she read and her own increasingly adventurous imagination.

The boys grew, Henry suffered. Hannah suffered.

Hannah was sad because she no longer had her babies and was left with Henry, for whom she felt the kindliness of long association but no passion. She had mistaken love, and neither she nor Henry was to blame, so she came to think that the honorable course was to try to subdue her longing for passion and settle for a quiet life. Except that it wasn't the honorable course, only the least effortful.

Henry was sad because now his sons admired him and he wanted his wife as well, but she was gone from him. She kept the house effectively and washed and cooked and carried out all her tasks, but he could never come close to her and she could never explain to him what beset her. After being guided and told what was best for her for so long, Hannah could not bring herself to have any belief in her own reasons and judgments and so could never risk coming to the point of trying to reach out to Henry. Anyway, he would be sure to start shouting and she was sure he would take all she had to say as criticism of himself. The explanations would emerge into sound as recriminations. She didn't know how you explained the growth of something huge without going back to the first tiny seed, and that meant going back to some tiny thing years ago, and that sounded like resentment deliberately harbored. It made her encompassing distress look like a fifteen-year sulk. And anyway, she knew she was likely to cry, quite without meaning or wanting to, and who can regard as weighty and rational an explanation delivered through hiccups?

If she had been able to crystallize her grievance, encapsulate it into a few exact words, they might have learned each other's language. Instead, they became foreigners to each other because words escaped Hannah. Her withdrawal from argument, silences, turning away, at first all inward, had gradually become outward, leaving Henry lonely, casting about helplessly for explanation, bewildered and seeing no fault in himself. He was the same as he always was. Why did Hannah have to change? So sweet, so shy once. Now a vague, distant woman who didn't like to be touched.

He went on with his research and began to write his history of garden statuary from the Greeks to the present day, dreaming continually, wishing he were Pygmalion to breathe life into Hannah, earnestly pursuing eccentric garden gnomes all over the home counties. His absurdity took on dignity, as fighting for a lost cause has dignity. The outcome is clear, but the principle commands admiration.

Hannah lived her dreams and dreamed her way through the days.

Life, that glittering prize, had slipped through her fingers when she thought she had it in her grasp and had got clean away. Not brave enough to order it back or run after it, she persuaded herself it was virtuous to make shift without it and to pass an orderly existence with Henry. In her pursuit of virtue she punished herself and Henry year after year after year.

Now, combing out her thoughts as she dresses, she sees herself at last for what she is. All Mrs. Owen's striving was in vain because Hannah recognizes that not only is she guilty of cowardice, but she is not a Nice Woman. On the contrary, she is full of rage and malice, which she has suppressed and ignored. Too late to undo past cowardice, it is very important to make her honest self known before this last chance slips away too.

Four

Bathed, combed, and made up, Hannah is going to a coffee-morning. For the first time ever, she anticipates it with some pleasure. She has never cared for covens but has obediently conformed and drunk coffee, bought plastic kitchenware and assorted jumble with a dismay she never recognized as fury lurking beneath her placid smile.

Today is different. It is the second day of the rest of her life. Yesterday, after lunch and the new hairdo, she went shopping. In the past she had made a practice of going to one particular store because it had mirrored pillars, and the mirrors, ever so slightly tinted and hung at just such an angle, are the most flattering she knows. It used to make her feel better to see her decent, respectable image faintly touched with gold and her nondescript skin take on interesting shadows.

Yesterday she gave up seeking support from dishonest mirrors.

She has no desire to look twenty again. Thinking back, she hates the idea of how she looked at twenty. It is unrealistic to attempt beauty because she doesn't have the foundation or the state of mind for that, and anyway one has to start young. But interesting is possible. It won't appeal to everyone, but what she wants now is to provoke positive reactions. So she had spent richly on cosmetics, glutting herself on colors, invoking the help of lady consultants, gleaming like new cars in a showroom, to show her how to suggest a hollow here, a contour there, and how to cause glances to slide, unnoticing, over this, to rest, noticing, on that. Each line and wrinkle that can't be erased must be turned to advantage. The unfamiliar result had affected her deeply. A face that was strange but one that she recognized immediately as someone she knew. It made her remember the surprise she had felt when her newly born first son was handed to her and she hadn't recognized him. Having shared mind and body with him for so many months she had quite expected the face to be familiar, and it wasn't, but this one looking out of the mirror was. A face with bones in it, cheeks and a jaw, instead of an approximate oval on a stalk. The new hair rose and swept back uncompromisingly from the new face, making no diffident gestures with little curls or wisps. And the hair was brown. Brown brown. No fancy name and no apology. She looked and recognized herself. The head was Hannah's.

So, wearing her new face and publicly displaying her nature, she embarks on the coffee-morning, without malice but intending to let honesty have some part in her behavior. She suspects that she is not alone in disliking the ritual gathering, but in this suburban culture-slide, if one misses two in succession one knows that one's reputation, housekeeping, husband, everything, will be picked through with surgical minuteness. So Hannah has sat, apparently placidly, silently disapproving, and not uttering her disapproval nor yet being brave enough to stay away.

It is Edith's turn to hold the coffee-morning at her house. Edith is big and handsome with a narrow, bony face and rather sinewy legs and a splendid bosom. Hannah, who has known Edith as a neighbor for fifteen years, has wistfully coveted Edith's bosom all that time, aware that the value society puts on a woman often grows in proportion to her cup size. It is the proud warmth of Edith's D cup combined with an episcopal voice that allows the authority she has assumed over her circle of acquaintances. Beside her, Hannah feels a wraith, sans bust, sans brio, sans substance even. It isn't

Edith's fault. She too has merely accepted the color and style in which her makers, husband, parents, custom, have painted her. Realizing this, Hannah is already, strolling to Edith's house, losing the urgent sense of her own uniqueness. Before she began fighting the source of her grievance, she had not considered the possibility of Edith's being the product of a similar molding. Edith's has been more enviable, designed to produce chairladies and felt-hatted magistrates rather than timorous Nice Women, that's all.

Edith's flamboyant mahogany hair, lushly recalling 1940 film glamour, quite unsuitably topping her expensively boring skirts and twinsets, now suggests itself to Hannah as a piece of bravado from Edith, showing she too is aware that she has been manufactured to someone else's specifications and is trying to make the presence of her self noticed.

We're like ghosts, Hannah thinks, rattling our chains to make ourselves manifest so someone will know we're here.

She feels a moment's sympathy for Edith, but it fades because she needs all her caring for herself and she doesn't much like Edith anyway on account of her managing ways and her bust.

Her arrival causes a chorus of oohs and aahs, followed by a moment's silence, which Edith naturally is the first to break.

"Hannah, dear, what have you done to yourself?"

Hannah revolves slowly in the circle of girls so they can all have a good look before she sits and accepts a cup of coffee.

"I had my hair done. What else? It goes up and back instead of down and forward, that's all."

"But your face is different," says one.

"Nonsense dear." Hannah smiles. "It's still my face as it always was."

They look at her suspiciously, sensing a difference apart from the one they see, suspecting that it's important. An air of unease hangs over the girls. Hannah has brought in with her something they don't understand. She is, in an undefined way, menacing as she sits so smoothly smiling with her new hair and new face. They know she has lied about her face.

The moment is broken by the late arrival of Betty Tracey, plumply invading the upholstered room, splashing down onto the settee, causing the other occupants to bounce gently and slop their coffee.

"Oh," she gasps, out of breath and full of news. "Coffee or I die, Edith. Sorry I'm late."

The girls stir. There is a promise in the atmosphere dispelling the unease of a minute ago. They dismiss Hannah for the moment. There will be another opportunity when she isn't there to discuss her. It will be delicious but it will keep. In the meantime, it is clear that Betty has brought them goodies.

They wait, a simmering quiet settling over them while Betty takes a sip of coffee, puts down her cup, fumbles for a cigarette, accepts a light, and then, blowing out a plume of smoke in the manner she has been cultivating since seeing a repeat of *Casablanca,* speaks.

"What do you think? I don't know what to think. Well, I do really. . . . Really . . . Sue's not here, is she? No, I didn't think she would be. Well, David's away on business. . . . I know that for sure because John gave him a lift to the station yesterday morning and he told him then that he was going to Birmingham for three days. Well, last night I was just putting out the milk bottles before going to bed, and there was a car near Sue's drive. I couldn't help seeing it, now could I?"

She pauses to receive the righteous assent that is her due and to take a sip of coffee.

"Yes," someone prompts. "Go on."

Betty moistens her pearly-pink lips with a sugar-pink tongue.

"It was still there this morning."

Silence.

"It was the same car. No doubt about that."

Silence then, while this morsel is ingested.

Edith speaks first.

"Brother?"

"She's an only child. She told me."

"Father?"

"Dead."

"Hmm. What's going on then, I wonder?"

Safety catch off. Don't jerk the trigger. Press firmly and steadily, that's what it says at the fairground rifle range.

"I expect," Hannah's voice says, clear and even and normal, while heads turn to look at her, impatiently anticipating a soothing, improbable possibility from reliable, boring Hannah, so good in an emergency, "I expect they were having it off on the settee."

Gasps. Ellen Evans's coffee goes down the wrong way and chokes her. It simply isn't done to say what you mean like that. Everyone knows what you mean without saying it out loud after all.

"Or even," Hannah continues, smiling a warm, encouraging smile, "on Sue and David's bed. That's a new settee. Pity to mark it."

She drinks her coffee and brushes a speck off her skirt.

The girls look at each other, disoriented. Their morsel has been taken from them. Who now can continue the conversation? Who can reverse this dreadful act of Hannah's? Everything is spoiled. The delicious promise of Betty's revelation has turned to ashes before they have done more than begin to taste the sweetness.

Edith speaks. It's Edith's house so in part Edith must share Hannah's odium.

"What can you mean, Hannah? What a shocking thing to say. It's not like you."

A chorus of agreement. Such a turbulence of feeling needs vocal expression. From the chorus a small solo voice: Elizabeth, newest bride, youngest woman, Hannah twenty years ago.

"Having it off? You don't mean . . ."

Hannah leans over and puts a kind hand on Elizabeth's arm.

"Having it off. Having it away. Fucking." She gives a deprecating little laugh. "Making love."

Elizabeth flushes and turns all aquiver to Edith for guidance. Edith puts an arm around Hannah's shoulders.

"Hannah, dear, you're not well. Would you like to lie down? Hmm?"

Over Hannah's head she mouths to the others, "Nerves. The Change."

"No thank you, Edith," Hannah replies. "I would not like to

lie down. My nerves are in splendid condition. I am not menopausal. I was merely saying what you all were thinking."

She rises. "Nevertheless, I shall go home now so you can all talk it over."

There is silence as she picks up her handbag. Edith makes no move to see her to the door. With her hand on the doorknob Hannah turns and smiles again.

"Edith. Dear. Thank you for the coffee. Menopausal though. You really must try not to give yourself away like that."

The front door shuts behind her with a hollow sound as if the house is empty now that she has left it. Perhaps it is, and they are all creatures of her imagination.

"I think, therefore I am," she murmurs, seeing what it means. Till now she has approached this concept from entirely the wrong direction, accepting the reality of the world, doubting her own. Now she is satisfied that her existence is a fact of itself, not an extension of other people's existences. If they are centers around which the world moves, then so, equally, is she.

Hannah Jackson. Woman, wife, mother, daughter, person. And on and on.

She sits in her quiet house and wishes it were summer. She is sad and disappointed.

She felt a short-lived delight at outraging the girls, but it was too easy and it's gone now. She wants to cry for them all, locked in their cages, pacing back and fore, their only release to snarl and now and then reach through the bars with a flashing of claws. Well looked after, cherished even, but locked up. She has seen that there is a way to unlock her cage. How petty to have stayed and snarled, when if she had truly cared about dignity she would have walked out and ventured into the world where, though she had not been trained for survival, she would at least have met the overpowering forces with honesty and pride.

She thinks of summer and the sun on her back. The sun has always helped her, warming away the aches in her mind like red flannel on a strained back, its immense presence cutting everything down to size. Perhaps it will be next year's summer that she dies. She would rather it weren't autumn . . . that would be too theatrical, to die as the leaves fell. No, summer would be much nicer. She does not mislead herself that she wants to die. Rather she wants to stop living her life. She can imagine circumstances where a woman of forty-two would be very anxious to go on living, but she's not. She hasn't been enjoying her life at all, she has botched it, and what she has decided upon is to stop doing something she feels she does badly and without satisfaction.

I suppose, she tells herself, considering the options again that she has gone through already, I could leave Henry, go away somewhere. Have the operation and make a new beginning, though beginnings are for the young. I suppose leaving Henry would be a decisive thing to do. He deserves a new beginning too. We've been very bad for each other!

She feels a surge of affection for Henry, forgives him the mess in the bathroom, repents the lack of crust on his bread. She is sad for Henry, working away at his book, pretending that it is the real reason for his days and hours away from her, not an escape from her resentful virtue.

She lights a cigarette and watches a plume of smoke rise to the ceiling and considers the possibility that she and Henry have been like two crabs, locked together in an empty place, each eating away at the other in order to survive instead of looking elsewhere for nourishment. Two crabs at least as malignant as the one quietly feeding on her now.

She won't change her mind. She is tired of herself, glutted with thinking about herself. She wants an end to it. Henry shall have his new beginning, and she will spend the rest of her time like the goat on the mountainside, rejoicing in the moment, in the knowledge that when the Wolf comes and fights her, he will win, but she will at least have had her day on the mountain.

Five

Henry is to be told. But as Hannah busies herself in her kitchen, preparing dinner, she wonders how. She peels onions, crushes garlic, shakes lettuce leaves. The meal will be soundly balanced nutritionally, good-tasting, low in cholesterol, everything Henry needs.

The approach to food, Hannah muses, can be an indication of character. It's no sensual experience for Henry. He has to eat, so he eats, and being the man he is, he requires good quality and durable results because that's the best value for his money and his well-being. Just like his suits, which are constructed of prime cloth and will last for years if properly cared for and as a consequence must be set apart from fashion. Dateless good taste, Henry calls it, an economy in the long run. Hannah thinks it may certainly be partly that, but there's a good measure of parsimonious dullness there too and a lack of spirit. No imagination. He likes his food very hot if it's supposed to be hot, cold if it's supposed to be cold, and no unidentifiable messes. He likes it served briskly without a lot of hanging about between courses, and of course it should nourish him and replenish his forces and not cause bad things to happen to his chemistry. Well, it's a point of view. Lots of people would give Henry full marks. But Henry's wrong all the same. He doesn't know food's a sensual thing, and it is.

Hannah cleans a spring onion, peeling off its outer skin delicately and feeling the slippery inner skin slide excitingly under her fingers. As she slips the outer skin off, she thinks again of satin knickers and regards the onion closely. It's so pretty, that pearly globe, changing so subtly into the beautiful little green stems. And who could guess that the jewel smoothness would taste like that? The bite and sting that come from the elegant roundness.

Hannah has been deprived. She wants to dine out, to luxuriate in a restaurant that charges unreasonable prices because it gives unreasonable pleasure. Her indulgence in food has been a spasmodic furtive escapade till now, the way her lunch the day before yesterday might have been if it had been any other day.

It seems such a silly business now. Silly is a silly word, just right for the silly game of avoiding Henry's bad humor at such cost both to her and to him. Being cross back would have been a more productive course. It might at least have precipitated a crisis, which would by some means or another have had an outcome by now. It would have been more worthy than waiting for this chance occasion without which she knows they would simply have drifted on until one or the other of them drifted disappointedly out of life.

A showdown. She tries the unaccustomed word and finds it unlovely but exact. We should have had a showdown. Now we shall have to have, are about to have, a showdown. Oh dear. I don't want all this agitation.

But this time, when she feels the quivering in her stomach and the hateful apologetic half smile, she considers them clinically, recognizes them as conditioned reflexes, and puts them to one side. No evasion. No need and no time. How to set about it though? How do you tell your husband that you're dying? Especially when you've lost the way of talking.

Hannah: Hullo. Did you have a good day at the drill, Henry? Filled lots of lovely cavities? Oh good. Guess what I've been doing. Dying. I've been at it all day. I haven't stopped for a moment. Carried on right through lunchtime.

That can't be the way, though Hannah finds it appealing. She imagines his reaction.

Henry: Oh? Well, never mind. Isn't dinner ready? I've had a difficult day. Very difficult.

End of conversation. Over dinner a gum-by-gum account of the day's hardships while Hannah waits for an opportune moment to slip in a remark about her troubles.

She sets the table, the dinner is ready. She puts out sherry and nuts. It will be a good thing, she decides, to have the showdown over the meal. It will give them something to do with their hands and faces while talking or listening or hurting each other, or trying to find a way to say things. Yes, that will be best.

When she hears Henry's key in the lock she is startled by the sudden dropping away of her stomach and the sick trembling of her knees. She feels like a little girl again, on the way back from the corner shop knowing she has to tell her mother that she's lost the change. It's just habit, she tells herself quickly, just habit, and it is, but the reaction is still there and it's very hard to compose her face and get her voice ready. She is no longer afraid of Henry in her mind or her feelings, but her body has twenty years of custom to overcome.

"Hullo," he calls.

"Hullo, Henry."

He comes into the kitchen and washes his hands, which are already aggressively clean. He sniffs.

"You've used a lot of garlic again."

"It's good for colds," she says mildly, leaning against the cooker and looking at him. You live with someone year after year and after a while you stop seeing him unless you make a positive effort to look. Like furniture. Hannah has a pale gray plastic bowl which she always thinks of as the red bowl because it was red when she first had it and the fading has been so gradual that it has quite escaped her notice. Henry is rather gray too, she sees. Distinguished, he'd call it, without further definition. He's kept enough hair to fluff out over his scalp and lost enough to be annoyed if caught out in the rain. He's broad and strong-looking, when dressed. The splendid cloth and cut of his suits corset him to some degree and help to maintain his inaccurate belief that he is fit. Casually dressed, he looks all wrong, uncomfortable, a shade embarrassed.

"I haven't got a cold," he says now.

"I might have, though."

"Have you?"

"No."

"Why bring it up then? Really, Hannah, you can be very irritating. It's not very nice to breathe garlic over one's patients."

She thinks of a dozen replies and says instead of any of them, "Sorry. It will be all right by the morning."

Grunting, Henry turns to go to the dining room.

Hannah calls, "Wouldn't you like a drink? I've put the sherry out in the living room."

"There's no one coming, is there? I didn't know there was anyone coming."

"I just thought it would be nice to have a drink before dinner."

He grunts a little, then decides he would enjoy a drink and smiles.

"Yes. That would be nice after a hard day."

Hannah follows him to the living room and pours two glasses of sherry. They sit, and the formality inhibits Henry. He fidgets for a moment, then relaxes and reaches for the newspaper.

"Henry?"

"Mmm?"

What to say? Is it the best moment? Best for whom? Henry? Hannah wants to say it now, so she says it now, though her hands are clenched and her neck feels rigid.

"Henry, will you listen, please."

"Mmm?"

"Henry, I'm going to speak to you. Please will you put the paper down."

The unusualness of the words and tone catches his attention.

"Something wrong? Overdrawn, I suppose. I wish you'd keep a better check on spending. However, I'll sort it out in the morning."

"I've got cancer, Henry."

There seems no way of being civilized about it.

Henry puts the paper down, folding it carefully first. He looks at his nails, pushes the cuticles back. The silence extends. The clock ticks more and more loudly. The room settles in around Hannah, each piece of furniture, each object becoming more and more sharply defined until all the hard edges are painful and she closes her eyes.

"Go on," Henry says at last.

"I have cancer of the cervix. It's been confirmed . . . there's no question of hysterical imaginings. I believe I have about two years, maybe a little less."

He jumps to his feet. He has of course a fairly extensive medical knowledge. He faces her with a mixture of love and relief and impatient annoyance.

"Hannah, Hannah. Two years? That means it's in its earliest stages. An operation and it'll be gone."

"I've decided against that."

His mouth drops open. He stops, frozen in mid-step toward her. Then he shakes himself a little and takes a deep breath.

"Oh, I see. X-ray treatment. For a moment I thought . . ."

"You thought right, Henry. I'm not going to have any treatment."

The air freezes.

"You can't do that. You can't *do* that. It's monstrous."

She merely looks at her lap.

"Monstrous. I insist you have the operation. I cannot allow you to kill yourself. It almost makes a murderer of me. There's no question of refusing treatment. None. I'll see to everything tomorrow, and . . ."

"I will no longer allow you to allow me or not allow me to do anything," she says and realizes that she has said it. The words are out. She has made a statement, drawn a line. It's a heady feeling. Not thrilling but profoundly relaxing. She feels a calmness descend on her and is quite sure that now she can see this talk through at her own pace without tears, taking time to get the words right. She is in control.

"If I want to," she continues, aware that she is taking a sneaky advantage, "I shall walk down the street with no clothes on, or shoplift at Woolworth's, or take a lover."

She settles back from the edge of her seat and sits comfortably. Henry stares. Who is this woman? How does he come to be involved in a mad conversation with a mad woman when all he has expected is his dinner and a quiet evening working on his book?

"You're mad," he shouts suddenly, waving his arms about. "Absolutely mad. Why should you want to take a lover, for God's sake?"

She bursts out laughing.

"Dear Henry." She gulps. "You'd give your blessing to the shoplifting, then. And the nude strolls."

"This is no time to be frivolous," he snorts, hunching his shoulders sulkily, feeling he has been ridiculous.

"On the contrary, it's the perfect time to be frivolous. How I long to be frivolous. Do the nonsense things I, we, should have done and didn't. Make love and laugh, play the silly games that lovers play."

He looks at her out of the corner of his eye, suspiciously. What does she mean? Is she mocking him?

"What do you know of the games that lovers play?" he asks.

"Very little. How could I know much? We were never lovers in the sense I mean. We coupled quite often, I know, in the early years, but so ineptly and without passion."

"I was passionate," he retorts at once, stung. "You were quite passionate too."

"No, that's not true. We were vigorous, yes, and showed some physical enthusiasm, but that applied just as much to your approach to cricket. You had some passion for that, I grant you. But not for me, truly. Not passion."

They look at each other and each sees a stranger. That makes it both better and worse. Better because it's easier to formulate objective arguments with a stranger, unhampered by the power to lay emotional traps. Worse because it's unnerving to be involved in such intimacy with a stranger. Hannah speaks.

"Our marriage really was an accident caused by circumstances and our upbringing. We've done quite admirably, I think, in view of that, but let's not be dishonest anymore and elevate it to a religious experience."

"Marriage is a religious experience. A sacrament."

"Not ours. Going through the motions, saying the words, that doesn't count for very much, not in the last resort."

Henry sits, and without covering his face he begins to cry silently. Hannah sees his tears with sympathy, with love even.

He says, tears honest on his face, "I've tried to do my best for you and the children. I've provided for you to the best of my ability, gladly."

"Yes, you have. You gave me safe ground to stand on, as you saw it, but we never compared our definitions of safety. You gave me housekeeping money and a house to keep with it. I gave you physical comfort, clean clothes, reliable meals. And we gave each other children. But where was the passion? The faith, hope, and charity? We've tried to fulfill everyone's ideas of ourselves and forgotten that we owe ourselves charity too. We should, I think, have paid more heed to our own ideas of ourselves."

He still weeps but he's listening too. There is a searching look on his face. He is following her thread, absorbing what she says and giving weight to it. She is tired of the physical effort of speaking but she must go on now that he is listening. She wants him to understand and not to feel blamed, because now, so quickly, she feels charity for him, honors his integrity, and fiercely wants them to be friends.

"Poor Henry," she sighs. "You know it too. We've been dishonest with each other. When we used to say 'I love you' what we meant was 'I'm stuck with you and wish to cause you no hurt because our situation is no more your fault than mine, but I wish, I wish, I were free.' Isn't that true, Henry?"

Sadly he nods.

"Well, don't be unhappy. Admitting it gives us some measure of freedom. To go or stay, either of us, and no need to make terms. I very much wish you to be happy, Henry."

"Go?" He looks up, startled, but with a spark that she recognizes immediately and gladly as hope.

"Henry, why don't we revert to nature, obey our instincts without regard to convention? It's man-made after all, so it's bound to be faulty."

He's struggling now. He knows there's a branch to catch hold of somewhere very near, to pull himself out of this deep water. He knows it's there and if he can find it he can pull himself to safety, but it's dark and he's confused and there is deep, dangerous water all around. He holds out his hands to Hannah.

"Hannah, help me."

Hannah is very careful. Loving warmth for Henry and, through his need, a sharp remembrance of her babies fill her. But there lies such danger. Before she knows it, she could be pulled back, willy-nilly, into the deep water with Henry, struggling again with him in the water instead of standing safe on the bank, guiding his hand toward the branch. Only because she has her feet on firm ground can she be of any use to them. She must not slip back.

"Do you remember that story I used to tell the boys? The one about the goat who wanted to be free, even though she knew that sooner or later the Wolf on the mountain would kill her. She couldn't help herself because it was her nature to live free, not to be kept in an enclosure, no matter how lovingly. So she ran away, and everything was marvelous until it got dark and then she was afraid. But even so, she wouldn't run back to her owner because even the most benevolent imprisonment was unthinkable after freedom, so the Wolf came and ate her up and it was all right because she'd known and agreed to the price beforehand."

"Morbid."

"The boys loved it. Joe even understood, I think. Tom just liked to hear about the goat getting her comeuppance, and the blood. Anyway, do you see at all what I mean?"

41

"I see you are drawing a parallel. I don't agree with it."

He gets up and paces the room heavily. He's a heavy man. To and fro he goes and Hannah closes her eyes because he disturbs the stillness, causing the air to churn.

"I don't agree, but I see there could be a parallel. I need to think."

"Good," she says, and leaves it at that, and they go and eat their dinner in a quiet, friendly way, talking of trivialities in an easeful manner that is novel for them.

Six

Hannah and Henry lie together in their marital bed. Hannah lies curled up in a fetal position, with a hand beneath her cheek. Henry, like a crusader on a tomb, feet together, hands folded piously on his bosom. It makes his nose stick up. The sleeping Henry had been a subject of much interest to Hannah in the first weeks of their marriage. She would prop herself on an elbow and stare at him, learning each plane and hollow, moving to each pore and follicle, resisting the temptation to squeeze the tiny blackheads that she observed from time to time. She had yearned over him, telling herself how much she loved him, pointing out to herself how her love was intensified by ticking off imperfections one by one and conscientiously not minding them. That proved how real her love was. Didn't it? It must be real love if she could smile indulgently and dismiss the incipient jowls and the too-small eyes as unimportant. That proved love, didn't it? She used to wonder whether he looked at her thus when she slept and did her best to sleep prettily just in case, chastised herself when she woke curled up, tousled, with messy hair and creases on her skin, or forgetfully scratched a waking itch. She asked him once, but he said, "Watch you sleeping? Don't be silly. What for?"

Gradually she stopped staring as none of the love seemed to seep through his skin like night cream and make him lovelier. She toyed with the idea of buying him a marvelous dressing gown with a waist and a long full skirt in some peacock fabric that shone dully in half light. Imagining him in it, she endowed him also with a dark predatory gaze and a long black moustache. But when she suggested a dressing gown as a present, he had delightedly chosen a cuddly homespun garment the color of a labrador, and indeed, once he was in it, the resemblance was inescapable.

Bedtime had withered into a ritual of teeth and alarm clocks, less and less surreptitious scratching, and worse.

Tonight she falls asleep at once, relaxed and soothed by the contact with Henry. Such an achievement, actually to talk to each other after so long. She wishes as sleep pours in around her that she could lie awake for a little while to get the full flavor of it.

Henry can't sleep. He feels calm, but under the calm he knows there is a gathering that sooner or later will come to a head and break out, and he wants, while the calm lasts, to think out his thoughts rationally. He will have to see this doctor of Hannah's. How could she go behind his back like that? It makes him seem uncaring or worse. What must the man think? He glances at Hannah beside him, fast asleep, and scolds her in his mind. You should have let me deal with all this, you shouldn't have meddled with things you don't know anything about, this is a serious business, not for wives to dabble with. Damn it all, why did you have to go behind my back like that, as if it were nothing to do with me, as if I weren't the one who makes decisions? You're not a child, you're forty-two, you should have known better. Hannah stirs in her sleep, turns over, smiles as if she has been listening to his thoughts, and he reconsiders them guiltily.

Could any of this estrangement there has been between them really have been his fault? He doesn't understand how. He has always been willing to treat her as a woman, to make love to her, if that was what she was going on about. It has been she who retreated from it, emotionally if not physically.

But was that what she was going on about? His brow creases, he has pins and needles in one hand. If she was unhappy, why didn't she say so? She had everything a reasonable woman could wish for. She had a good house, two splendid sons, himself. What fairy froth had she been hankering after? His mother would have been more than content with such riches. He turns his thoughts to his mother to see if he can find some point that will explain why she had been so content while Hannah evidently has not. Involuntarily he smiles when he thinks of his mother in a patient, impatient, protective, ir-ritated way. What a dear little thing she is, one really can't blame her for her shortcomings. Of course she fusses. She hasn't been used to dealing with things. She married straight from home and Henry's father, the late Mr. Jackson, had seen to it that she never had to worry about anything thereafter, beyond what color curtains to choose and suitable feminine things like that. How many times has he thought, biting his lips in irritation, that his mother, that Hannah, ought to have his problems, to make them realize what life was really all about.

And how many times does he remember his mother speak-ing to his father thus: "Leonard, the vicar's wife let something slip today that you'd told the vicar that business was very bad. Is it, Leonard? Won't you tell me about it? Is business really bad, Leonard? Because I'm sure I could economize if it would help. Leonard?"

And his father patting her impatiently on the head and say-ing: "Nothing for you to worry about, dear. You leave that to me, there's a good girl."

And Hannah: "Henry, are they really demolishing the whole block where your consulting room is? What will you do? Shall I start going around to some real estate agents? It would save you doing it."

And himself: "You wouldn't know what to look for, Han-nah. I'll see to it myself. Don't you worry."

Henry moans silently. I meant to protect her. I only did what father taught me to do. Is that what's been gnawing at her?

What on earth has she got to bring goats into the question for? Surely she couldn't mean that she considered herself tethered, that he kept her in some sort of prison, such a prison that death was preferable? Pain expands in Henry's head. He loves her, so sweet, so shy, so pretty. He turns his head and looks at her and even in the half light he sees now that she isn't pretty at all. The apple rosy freshness has gone without trace. A thin middle-aged woman is sleeping beside him. When did it all happen? Where was the first grain that grew into this ghastly confusion? Surely this marriage started off as well, even better, than most? They didn't have any financial struggles. He had been tolerably well established before he met Hannah. She had moved straight into circumstances that most brides waited for for years. He had been an established man, with a ready-made establishment, and she hadn't had to struggle for a thing.

Now she tells him he's been wrong, destructive. He is accused and doesn't understand the charge, so he can't see how to defend himself. What has his crime been? To do, conscientiously, what he thought he was required to do? How else can an honorable married man, a husband, a father, conduct himself? Can it be wrong to safeguard and guide smaller people, less able to bear weight than himself?

His sons . . . surely he's not culpable in their case. He's neither an unapproachable nor a clinging father. They're grown up and he lets them live their lives without interference. But when they were little boys, they were his charge and he fulfilled it, and he recognized that a time came for them to leave the shelter of his paternity and be responsible for themselves.

He's done that right. He's sure he's done that right.

Henry rolls his head heavily on the pillow as he follows the thought through.

What if they had been girls, his children? What then? Would he have behaved in the same way, let them leave and be separate from him, at risk, standing out in the cold world without his body between them and the wind?

Now a spider's thread of recognition is forming. No. Daughters, wives, mothers, they are not, in Henry's picture of the way things are, to be expected to withstand cold winds. They are frail. They're not brought up to it. Boys are. That is the order of things. That is what his father taught him, by word, by example, by his whole manner of conduct.

But Hannah . . . is what she's saying that she doesn't want, never wanted, to be cared for? Not in the way he has cared. But it's the only way he knows. Is she saying that what he calls care, she calls exile from life? That what he thinks of as a pretty, secluded garden, she thinks of as a pen? Now Henry sees where goats come into the question. He's a good, kind man, Henry. He suffers, and blames himself, and blames Hannah too for not forcing this issue, though he understands how her nature and his made it next to impossible. He looks at Hannah and feels a protective love almost clean of the stain of possession. Could they start again? She could have the operation. They could talk until each was confident of the other's understanding, and then a new marriage could begin. They could move to a new neighborhood even. They could go right away. They could do anything. Henry with increasing desperation piles up more and more possibilities to delay admitting the fearful fact that he has to admit: Hannah's body, now that it carries destruction in it, a gnawing, creeping, consuming thing, is repellent to him. He can never again—even though the crab is cut out and burned and the body made clean and whole—he knows he can never bear to make love to Hannah again.

He closes his eyes in anguish. He is bitterly ashamed and wants to cry on Hannah's breast and be comforted and have his hurts kissed better. Dear God, he thinks, is there a way through this? Hannah stirs, opens her eyes, and sees him. She puts her hand on his.

"It's all right, Henry. It will be all right. You'll see. Go to sleep."

And he does.

But she wakes. Wide awake, she lies beside Henry, her hand firm and warm on his. Hold Mummy's hand, dear, while we cross this dangerous road. She wants him to be safe, to know the rules of the road so that he can go into the big world able and confident when the time comes. She feels paradoxically that they are young people who have just met and have eons to grow up together, and that he is someone else's child whom she must take care of and give affection to temporarily.

It is evidently not as easy as she had thought, this simple living of the rest of one's life. Perhaps she should go into a convent, retreat now, remove herself from the field of play. But that would make a nonsense of her determination. Shouting petulantly, "I'm not playing anymore, so there," that's not living, conducting oneself with grace and style. Besides, she wants to profit from this.

She is surprised at the sudden need she feels for some good to attach itself to her, some reward or benefit for being such a good brave girl. What's in it for me after all? she asks, because dignity and decision-making are turning out not to be enough. What more? All the things she's missed. That's not realistic. Well, some of them, then. What she said to Henry . . . the games that lovers play . . . that had been unconsidered, a trifle tossed off thoughtlessly, but Hannah thinks now she may by accident have said something significant, thrown up from her subconscious mind. What if, somewhere in the world, there is a soul mate for Henry and one for Hannah, undiscovered? How appealing the old concept of half people wandering about searching for their matching other half to make themselves whole. Poor other halves, condemned without so much as a by-your-leave to remain halves forever and ever. Poor Henry and Hannah, stuck with their mistakes, trying to make disparate halves join and ending not with a smooth, lovely whole, but with an inelegant grinding of gears. Hannah's eyes fill with tears for all four halves, destined never to get the puzzle right. She sees herself, wearing a long, narrow black gown covered with sequins and making serpentine movements around a microphone, hoarsely singing into blue smoke a melancholy song about separated lovers. Then she sniffs and smiles at herself and such mawkish ramblings. She should go peacefully to sleep or get up and make a cup of tea or read a book.

But later, if it happens that she can't sleep, and can't get up, how will it be then? A tremor of fear makes her squeeze Henry's hand and he grunts but doesn't wake. How is it going to be, after all, when she is obliged to carry through the final part of her determination? It will be too late then for changes of heart or mind. Will she then cling to Henry, begging him to take charge and worry about everything and reproduce the quiescent Hannah and the lordly Henry and the way things were?

Death is messy and it smells and is not in the least graceful. Even La Dame aux Camélias and Juliet and Ophelia probably died open-mouthed with a graceless evacuating of bowels. Even those terminal horrors don't compare though with the slow approach to them. Hannah thinks of her mother. For the first time in her adult life, she wants her mother, needs that granite support. Mother died magnificently, she remembers with pride. Even at the time, Hannah was filled with awed admiration and afterwards had been profoundly shaken by the extent of her mourning.

Mrs. Owen had not after all lived forever. She had died with the same steely resolve with which she had lived, but a steel polished and shaped into magnificence, transcending the assaults on her dignity and modesty and the monstrous intrusions on her independence.

Oh no, Hannah pleads, not all that. Not like Mother. Not the anguished eyes full of consciousness and will, suffering in the helpless body that all the will in the world could not make respond. The dignity of the near-useless hand triumphantly trailing a cloth to the flaccid mouth, ineffectually but superbly to mop at the uncontrollable dribbling. The splendor of uninvolvement when her defenseless limbs were exposed and washed and, at the end, when Hannah in the interminable night knelt beside her and at last loved her.

Hannah spoke to her in the waiting nights, half asleep herself, talking on and on at first to still the silence, later to try to fill the empty spaces in their knowing of each other. And one night, the windows black against the void outside, Hannah, crouched in the dim pool of light around the bed holding her mother's hand, stopped her soft spiel and whispered urgently, "Mother, please die," and Mrs. Owen struggled until she made her damp mauve mouth obey and her eyes glow with determination, and answered, "I'm trying to, Hannah."

I can't do it like that, Hannah cried inwardly. I don't have courage like that. That's the way it ought to be done and I'll make a filthy mess of it. I'll cry and wail and make everyone want me to die to give themselves relief from me, not to spare me suffering. Oh God, oh Mother, help me. Make me do it right. What if I can't when it comes to the point?

Her mind starts to spin. Mother ironing, Mother with set, angry mouth, Mother telling the world to stop bullying her because she knew how to deal with bullies, Mother meltingly soft with Hannah's babies and gradually stiffening into imperious grandmotherhood as they grew up. All of it adding up to Mother declaring her uncompromising self, right through her life. Now Hannah understands, now that she herself is trying to make her voice heard. Mrs. Owen often used to talk of her own mother and the shame of the slavish life she led, a skivvy in her husband's house, kept short of money, and a baby every year. It's clear now—Mrs. Owen wouldn't, couldn't, settle for that, so she assumed power and made herself grow to fit it, forcing onto Mr. Owen the alternative role she was refusing for herself. Henry's mother gave in to circumstances and made her cage cozy and cuddled down into it. Mrs. Owen fought against them and the war went on forever, with many casualties. Then which way am I going, Hannah wonders. I've tried one and it was wrong for Henry and for me. Now I'm trying the other, but it's probably too late, it's like trying to climb on a carrousel when it's whirling around. Tom, Joe, what shall I do? I don't have a daughter to kneel beside me and hold my hand and make it all just a little bit easier to do. If I explain to you, will you be able to help me, or will you dismiss me impatiently as a nuisance, and anyway does any of this count if I arrange beforehand like this not to do it alone? No, think back to the day before yesterday and the brave certainty then. Hang on to that. I will do it right. I will be afraid but I will not cry and wail and no one but me shall know what I'm thinking. The Wolf is just a big bully. It threatens everyone because it's big and strong. So when it comes, I'll fight it for a while and then steal its thunder by doing it right at the end.

A sleepy calm falls on her.

Here we lie, Henry and I, not guilty. We didn't do it, my Lord. It was our mothers and fathers and their mothers and fathers, from the beginning forever and ever, Amen.

Hannah sighs and falls asleep.

Seven

This morning Hannah wakes happily. She has always been intrigued by sleep and waking. As a child she used to lie snugly
in a nest-warmth, waiting to fall asleep and determined to stay
awake while she did it so that she could find out exactly what
happened. In the mornings, she would be mildly exasperated
that she hadn't managed it and would try again, but it always
slipped away from her. Waking she would find herself again
and ponder: Where have I been? I was lying here but I, the
thinking I, wasn't. How does it happen? As if the thinking
part had been turned out like a light. It made her nervous to
think how easily her consciousness could be extinguished and
her body left unoccupied and defenseless. Was that what
dying was like? Such questions have continued, intermittently,
to concern her, and now she has a more immediate interest in
formulating answers.

This morning, though, the sun is shining fitfully and a
gusty wind is fluttering the curtains. It's a small but intense
pleasure to lie warm and comfortable and feel a cool wind
blowing across her face.

She hears sounds downstairs. Henry is already up. Surpris-
ingly, he is singing. An out-of-tune, inaccurate mumble-sing-
ing of the *Ride of the Valkyries*. Hannah smiles though the

inaccuracies grate on her. It's a lovely morning. The world hasn't disappeared during the night. And what day is it today? It takes a moment to gather all the bits and pieces of scattered consciousness together. It must be Thursday. Oh dear. Tonight, Thursday night, Edith has a dinner party and Hannah and Henry are required to attend. Or perhaps not, after the coffee-morning. She had forgotten the dinner invitation during the coffee-morning. She will have to do something about it. Well, never mind. Hannah uncharacteristically puts Edith and her dinner to one side. Later on will be soon enough to think about it.

Henry's footsteps on the stairs, the *Ride of the Valkyries* getting closer. He comes in carrying a cup of tea.

"Oh, you're awake. I've brought you some tea."

"That's nice. Thank you."

She sits up and Henry stands watching her while she takes a sip of her tea. He wears his labrador dressing gown, not the original newlywed one but the latest in a line of identical replacements. His feet are bare and his big toes have tufts of hair on them. A Hobbit, thinks Hannah. Henry the Hobbit with furry feet. She bends her head hurriedly to her cup. Henry wouldn't think it was funny. He might even be offended. He would think it a criticism of his big toes and worry at it. They are both rather embarrassed.

"It looks like a nice day," she says.

"Yes. Quite sunny. A bit of a wind."

"Oh good."

She sips more tea, smiling too naturally at Henry, who nods and smiles back.

"What time is it?"

"About half past seven. There's no rush."

"Oh good."

She finishes the tea and doesn't know what to do next, but still feels happy.

"I'll go and shave, then."

"All right."

He nods again and turns to go and the movement breaks the awkwardness.

"Henry?"

"Yes?"

"I'm glad we talked yesterday. It made me feel a lot better."

"Yes. Yes, I'm glad too. I couldn't sleep for a while last night. Thinking, you know. We should have cleared the air a long time ago."

"We should, but now we have and I feel quite, well, uplifted."

"That's good. So do I, as a matter of fact. Well, I'll go and shave."

He shuffles toward the door and stops. Without turning to look at her, he says, "You will have the operation now, won't you?"

Hannah is silent, Henry waits.

"I don't think so, Henry."

He makes no reply, just stands still for a minute with his back to her before he goes quietly out and to the bathroom. Hannah's little happiness shakes, then settles again. Of course it will take some time. Henry can't be expected to accept her design wholesale just like that. He's a prudent man. Already he's been more amenable, touchable, than she had thought possible. The showdown that she had anticipated as a nasty melodrama had, thanks to Henry, been more than tolerable. It had been therapeutic. She is grateful to him. It would be churlish at this point to stifle any comment he wants to make. He's bound to try to persuade her. It's the conventional thing to do and convention is what Henry lives by. Time enough to draw lines when she runs out of time to spare.

"Henry?" she calls, getting out of bed.

"Mm?"

"We're supposed to be going to dinner at Edith's this evening."

"I'd forgotten. Right ho."

She brushes her hair, turning her head this way and that to admire her new cheekbones, liking the lift of hair from her temples.

"Henry?"

"Yes?"

"I went to Edith's for coffee yesterday." She walks along the landing, wrapping her version of the labrador dressing gown around her. It's a woolly blue like, as Henry remarked with pride when he gave it to her, Christopher Robin's Nanny's.

She leans at the bathroom door. Henry, lathered, is making faces at himself in the mirror while drawing a razor over his skin, making a rasping sound.

"That must be horrid to do every day," she comments.

"No worse than putting all that stuff on like you do."

"I was rude at Edith's yesterday."

She waits. He carries on shaving, holding the tip of his nose and pulling it up until his nostrils are vertical. She wants him to do something about Edith so that she won't have to, but as soon as she thinks it she's cross with herself. Why on earth should he? It's her little mess, she must clear it up. But the habit of passing every buck to Henry, on his advice, is so deeply ingrained.

"Rude?" Henry asks, his chin high in the air as he scrapes dangerously at his Adam's apple.

Hannah pulls her belt in firmly.

"I said 'fuck,' " she states bleakly.

Henry gives his neck a further scrape, then he turns to her.

"You said 'fuck,' " he repeats.

Hannah looks at her bare feet. Her big toes aren't hairy, she notes. They're rather nice altogether, no bunions, no corns. She remembers reading somewhere that the Chinese consider feet very erotic.

"Mm."

Henry starts to laugh. He laughs and laughs. He sits on the lavatory seat and grabs a towel and clutches it to him in rapture. Hannah stares at him. Henry doesn't laugh like this. Unrestrained laughter embarrasses him. After a little while, when his guffaws are beginning to abate, she says querulously, "I don't think it's funny."

He nearly starts again, but pulls himself together and stands, patting his face with the towel.

"I'm sorry," he says, "it's merely that I've been suppressing a desire to do that very thing for years, to dash in like Attila the Hun when all you girls are sitting there like so many self-righteous marshmallows and shout all the naughty words I can think of."

Hannah's mouth drops open.

"Henry."

She stares at him. This isn't Henry, is it, confessing to naughty secret longings, laughing out loud? She didn't know he could. She sits down on the edge of the bath. Now she comes to think of it, they never have laughed much together. Or cried or argued. They haven't been fit to be in charge of a marriage. She still stares at Henry and the dressing gown. Together they make a shapeless hairy golden brown mess, and she resists an impulse to pat them kindly and tells herself to stop wandering. She ought to be concentrating on the matter at hand. Edith, what to do about Edith? She gives a sudden snort of laughter.

"You should have seen them. So complacent. Such good women. They thought I'd lost my mind."

Henry pats aftershave lotion on his cheeks and looks levelly at her.

"Well, you have, haven't you?"

Laughter ends.

"I'll go and make breakfast."

She turns to go, but he reaches out and puts his hand on her arm.

"Hannah, Hannah. This is important. Don't let's stop talking. Don't let's stop and think before we speak."

She relaxes again, leans against him even.

"Yes. It's habit, you see. Exactly what I was trying to explain before."

"I know. We've been running on tracks. Anyway, don't worry about Edith. It might make the evening quite fascinatingly different."

She hums the *Ride of the Valkyries* as she goes downstairs and starts making breakfast. From upstairs she hears an occasional chuckle from Henry as he moves about, dressing. Though she is a bit nervous about facing Edith, she is cheered by Henry's attitude and appreciates his not taking the matter out of her

56

hands and sorting it out. It shows a sensibility she has assumed he didn't have.

When he comes down, he is Henry as before, stiff-collared,
dark-suited, armored in formality.

"Right," he says briskly, as he does every morning, and eats
his breakfast efficiently. Hannah regards him over the rim of
her coffee cup, wondering whether his upstairs behavior, so
out of character, was a flash in the pan, shock, whatever.

He finishes his coffee, rises, pulls down his waistcoat, rinses
his hands at the sink. Hannah watches with bush baby eyes
over her cup.

"Give me this doctor's name and number," he says firmly,
and as it is only fair, Hannah complies. But when he is about
to leave the house she says in a way meant to be equally com-
manding, though it has a nervous edge to it, "Speak to him by
all means, I do see you have the right, but neither of you is to
try and arrange any sort of plan for me. I will not be manipu-
lated anymore."

He stands in the doorway and looks at her as if he hasn't
seen her for a long time, then unexpectedly he puts his hand
on her cheek.

"All right. I must talk to him. But then we, you and I, shall
have to think of what's to be done."

She nods, satisfied.

"I'm off then. I'll be back about six, I think. What time at
Edith's?"

"Seven-thirty. I'm a bit scared." Still a part of her wants him
to be lordly and solve it for her.

He smiles, startling her. He and the old Henry keep switching. She's not sure which one to expect from second to second. But then, she admits, he is faced with a quandary equal
to her own. It needs time and talk and charity. And all of
these are available. No need to force the pace, just a need to
watch where they put their feet and be sure the ground is
solid before trusting to it.

"Why don't you get yourself a new dress? Present from
me."

"Well, thank you, Henry. I might."

"Hmm. 'Bye then." And he's gone, leaving a flurry in the air as after the passage of a car.

Hannah trails back to the kitchen and sits at the table, overcome by strangeness and the vacuum of the day ahead. Her waking mood has evaporated and she feels as if she's been up and about for hours. Should she get dressed first or wash the dishes or phone Edith? It all seems a very great deal to do. Decisions to make. Very tiring. She sits and waits for answers to come to her. They don't, and after a while she rises heavily, tucking Nanny's dressing gown more snugly around her. Ugh. "It's a beautiful blue, but it hasn't a hood, God bless Hannah and make her good." She hates this dressing gown. There. There's an answer. Get out of this horrible, beautiful blue garment, then she'll feel better. Purposeful now, she goes upstairs and dresses, makes the bed, straightens the bathroom. Oh yes, she feels better. She will give the dressing gown away this very day. It's been sapping her, it's symbolic, blue never was her color and besides, it makes her look like a stuffed toy. Out with it.

She rinses dishes briskly, whisks the kitchen into order in moments, and forces herself to the telephone before the thought occurs to her: Why speak to Edith at all? If Edith doesn't want her to go to dinner, Edith must put her off. Dear me, she's nearly done it again, nearly tried to make everything nice for everyone at her own expense, nearly made it easy for Edith, nearly supplied the girls with a dinner-table topic that would keep them happily engaged until the men were ready to indulge them with a few crusts cut off from the edges of their conversation.

I'll get used to it, Hannah tells herself, backing away from the telephone. I'll get into the way of it quite soon. She goes upstairs and carefully but more flippantly than yesterday puts on her face, parcels up the dressing gown for the Salvation Army, and sets out to view dresses suitable for Dinner at Edith's.

Eight

In Edith's house at seven o'clock there is discomfiture in the air. More than that. Edith is nervous and because she's nervous, she's cross. She blames it on Hannah. Hannah is really being most inconsiderate. Not a word of apology or explanation. Not a word at all. It is too bad. Had she only had the grace to grovel a little, Edith would have had the satisfaction of being magnanimous, which would have put her in a very good humor. Can Hannah really be intending to come? Perhaps she will simply not turn up, and then Edith will have a cast-iron grievance. She will also have two helpings of everything left over and whereas nothing will go to waste, not in Edith's house, it will naturally be a reinforcement of grievance. And what about Henry? Does he know? Ought she maybe to drop a delicate hint in his direction about Hannah and nerves?

She tuts and fusses as she makes final adjustments to the table and checks the food, her mouth grimly set, her already painted face incongruous and clownlike under her hair that is wound up on giant rollers ready to be released at the last moment. She wears a housecoat over her slip and her husband, Cyril, finds her offensive to look at. Why must she so thoughtlessly inflict all the preparatory scaffolding on him in order later to display the finished structure to other women and their husbands? She'll sit there later, Queen Bee, all polish and enamel, queening it over those silly women and their boring husbands, and they'll all drink his drink and eat his food and as soon as they're gone, Edith will dismantle herself and he'll be left with the bills and the washing up and the basic penny-plain Edith. He sulkily decants his medium-priced sherry into the bottles with expensive labels that he keeps for the purpose. He knows the girls will sip it with exaggerated appreciation, agreeing eagerly with each other that yes, quality shows, yes, doesn't it, and they'll know he's swapped bottles because that's what they do too and he knows they know, and they know he knows. Playing idiotic games, thinks Cyril, uneasily casual for home entertaining in his smart trousers and neckerchief. What a way for grown-up people to behave.

Whatever happened to Friends? Where did they go? He used to have friends. He used to be a friend. Now he entertains, and why? Because Edith sets it up. Because it's expected. Because you have to do it back when it's been done to you. Cyril is sad in a bad-tempered kind of way which is a pity because he really is a very nice man. Nice in the way Henry is nice. He likes Henry, as a matter of fact, and doesn't really mind Henry's drinking his whisky and knowing about the sherry, because Henry is meticulous about returning hospitality, and he's a good chap generally. They can talk easily enough together while the girls are clattering away to each other, nineteen to the dozen the way they do about their absorbing little nothings.

He and Henry have quite a lot in common, both professional men, both bill-paying machines, keeping up a pyramid of appearance. But it's not like Friends used to be, when he was young, sharing, caring, not competing, not playing dishonest games. Still, Henry's a good chap and Hannah's a good, quiet little thing, colorless, but restful. Easier to like than the other girls, much. Nice woman. Not bossy like Edith, Henry's lucky there. Cyril and Edith both know that Cyril is master in his own house, but Cyril does have occasion to remind Edith rather often. He imagines that Hannah is more docile, compliant, knows more how to treat a man.

"Are you ready, Cyril?" Edith's voice is strident. She appears at his side, nudging him away from the drinks table with her elbow while she surveys the bottles and glasses. He glances at her, observes the rolled-up hair that has jerked her eyebrows up with it into an unfortunate, amazed expression, and closes his eyes briefly. He reaches for the whisky but Edith is there before him.

"You don't need a drink now," she informs him tersely.

Cyril looks at her, the hair, the paint, the twenty-five years of his life she represents, the lost illusions, the long-gone friends. Then he takes the whisky from her.

"I am going to have a drink now," he says softly. "It may well be the first of many."

Edith recognizes the tone. She steps back and starts taking pins out of her rollers.

"I'm going up to see to my hair then," she says. "I really think I'd rather not be down when the Jacksons come. That is, if she has the effrontery to come."

He looks questioningly at her.

"What's she done? Hannah Jackson wouldn't say boo to a goose."

"She said 'fuck' to me."

Cyril takes a deep draught of whisky. In his mind's eye he sees Hannah, not in much detail because Hannah has never been memorable, but as a vague impression of grays and fawns with eyes. It seems he must rethink Hannah.

"Fuck," says Cyril, as he might repeat a name he has just been told.

"You don't have to enjoy it, Cyril," says Edith, turning away, her hands full of rollers and pins, her hair hanging absurdly around her face.

"Tell me more," invites Cyril, topping up his whisky glass, suddenly feeling much more cheerful and following Edith from the room. In their bedroom Edith begins to brush out her hair and it crosses Cyril's mind, fleetingly and not for the first time, that he would probably never have thought of marrying her at all if he hadn't had a well-brought-up young blood's false impression that women with cascades of red hair must thrash about a lot on white sheets, flames of hair obscuring faces distorted by passion. He has mourned that illusion more than most of the others.

Edith relates Hannah's iniquity, skillfully fading out the context. Cyril gravely listens, nodding wisely, giving his solemn attention. So attentive, so solemn, that Edith becomes suspicious and her indignant recital falters from a flood to a trickle to drips to a halt.

Cyril chews his whisky, looks into it as if it were a crystal ball, while Edith looks at him, her hairbrush in her hand, wondering, anxious.

"Well?" she asks.

"I hope she enjoyed it," Cyril says. "It's such an enviable thing to have done that it would be a shame not to have enjoyed it."

Edith is so cross she stamps her foot. Cyril is delighted. The evening has taken on promise.

"When you do that, Edith," he says, coming to her where she stands panting in temper and cupping her shoulder in the palm of his hand, "when you do that"—Edith stares at him in confusion—"it makes your boobs wobble. You might tip over." He pats her shoulder and quietly leaves the room, still nodding wisely, as the doorbell rings.

He hopes it will be Henry and Hannah because there must be depths to the story that it would be diverting to plumb, but it's a couple he doesn't recognize. Damn Edith. She should have told him who was coming, or he should have asked. She used to say he never entered into the spirit of entertaining and he used to tell her just to get on with it if she must, but not to expect enthusiasm from him, so now she does just that and he pays and quite enjoys it from time to time in spite of himself and supposes it keeps her happy. Meanwhile here he is standing at his door facing an unknown couple who have evidently come to eat his food in his house.

"Well hullo," he says heartily. "Come along in. Now you're

not the Jacksons, and you're not the others, so you must be . . ."

"The Howards." The woman breaks in, as he had counted on, in a pleasant amused tone that makes him suspect she knows the rules of this sort of game.

The man shakes hands with Cyril. Their eyes are on a level, but whereas Cyril gives an impression of weight and breadth, this man suggests height and slenderness.

"David Howard," he introduces himself, "and this is Christine. We moved in, down the road, a couple of weeks ago."

"Ah yes," says Cyril, quite pleased to see new faces and in a high good humor now.

It's not going to be a standard evening. He will drink rather a lot, maybe stir things up a bit, and go into the office late in the morning. He's paying, why shouldn't he enjoy it.

He sees to drinks, making the usual chat, saying Edith's just coming, and Christine smiles at him, warm but not provocative, no coquette this one. He's glad she's seeing him for the first time on his home ground. New faces are rather rare in this society. Edith billows in in her white silk caftan, bosom first, looking, thinks Cyril with mildly affectionate meanness, like the winner in the Tall Ships race.

"Christine, dear," she cries, hands outstretched, leaning across her bosom to offer her cheek. "And this is David? Oh my goodness, what an asset you're going to be, David. We're so awfully short of attractive men."

She smiles magnificently at him, holding his hand in both of hers.

"Don't monopolize his whisky hand, old dear," says Cyril, thrusting a glass at David.

"Mother here always wanted a boy, didn't you, Mother?" he adds naughtily, and Edith contrives to glare at him without letting her smile slip. She careens across to Christine again and they sit on the sofa side by side, Edith making a practiced move which lifts the caftan to her knees because she has an inexplicable conviction that her sinewy legs are much admired.

Cyril and David go through the opening moves of the male-first-meeting dance, with its attendant chorus of ohs and ah-yeses and ha-has.

The doorbell rings again. The Dawses. George and Janet. George booms in, rubbing his hands, swooping to peck Edith's cheek, "Who's a gorgeous bird, then," and moving on to Christine, "Don't know this little lady yet, but give me time, give me time." He's a nice man too, is George, but his shyness has mixed uneasily with his paradoxical success as a salesman and has confused him. He talks loudly, with daunting cheerfulness, hears himself doing it and can't stop, overwhelms his wife with the vigor and unimagination of his coupling because he has never been brave enough or unembarrassed enough to talk to her about it, and wishes without hope that things could change. Janet nods along behind him like a toy on a string, smiling, smiling. She takes such good care of him, watches his weight, counts his cigarettes, denies him butter, encourages him to exercise, all to try and purge herself of her guilty dreams of an early coronary for him, followed by a peaceful, solvent widowhood for her, undisturbed by loud jokes and distasteful encounters in the dark of her bed.

George joins the dance. Janet sits on the sofa.

Janet knows there will be another couple to complete the party. Everyone else in the circle invites to dinner two couples at a time. Edith has to have three because she's Edith and has her position to maintain.

"Are we last?" inquires Janet circumspectly.

Edith spreads her hands in helpless supplication.

"My dear, do you know, I'm not sure? The Jacksons were to come, but I haven't heard a word from either of them, though in the circumstances . . ."

"Oh dear," says Janet.

Christine looks from one to the other.

"You would have thought, wouldn't you . . ." says Edith.

"Oh yes. You would," says Janet.

"Something wrong?" asks Christine. She has a trace of an American accent.

Edith half turns toward her. Janet does the same. She is enclosed by them as in brackets.

"There was a rather unfortunate little happening yesterday when I had some friends here for coffee. Somebody behaved rather badly." She looks sadly down at her hands in her lap.

"Of course, among friends, one can be frank, but there are limits, and in my experience, which is quite wide, a woman of status can safely leave certain words out of her vocabulary."

Janet nods agreement. Christine looks interestedly amused.

Edith is about to continue when the doorbell rings again, making her start dramatically. She presses a hand to her bosom and looks in wide-eyed appeal at Cyril.

"That'll be Banquo's ghost," he says, exchanging a matey glance with George, who says "ha ha," and with David, who smiles and raises his eyebrows. They freeze into still life as Cyril goes to the door and they turn and talk to each other, listening over their shoulders.

"Hullo, Henry, old man. Nice to see you. Hannah, hullo. Hannah, hull-ooh."

Edith and Janet nearly stop talking, their ears twitch, but they succeed in sitting still.

Hannah comes in, Cyril's arm around her shoulder. She has said nothing yet. Henry follows. Edith rises and holds out her hand to Hannah, bravely borne hurt conspicuously concealed in the greeting.

"Hannah dear," she says and presents her cheek. Hannah aligns hers briefly.

"Edith, how handsome you look."

Edith is a tiny bit mollified, but doesn't allow herself to enjoy the compliment because it's not enough and Hannah hasn't groveled, seemed out of countenance, or even kissed her cheek deferentially. Introductions are made. Eyebrows signal vigorously between Janet and Edith and attempt to include Christine, who either cannot or will not respond.

Henry, passing Hannah with a touch on her shoulder, joins the men. Handshakes, talk of cars and golf. The men are standing in a group near the drinks table, and well apart from them sit three women in a row on the sofa. Hannah stands alone, wearing a tube of earth-brown jersey, high to her neck, long to her wrists, with a dull sheen of silk. A dress that says, "I am putting my cards on the table," but is lying in saying it.

Edith pats the last space on the sofa, inviting Hannah to sit. Cyril turns from the organization of drinks and looks at the tableau.

"Hannah," he booms, "what are you drinking? Sherry, isn't it?"

"Gin please, Cyril." Hannah smiles. "It's quicker, isn't it?"

Cyril takes his hand away from the sherry and pours a large gin. Edith and Janet watch with close attention. Christine calmly sips the sherry she was given. Cyril comes across and gives Hannah her glass and looks at her with more perception than he is usually given credit for.

"There you are, my love. It is quicker if you're in a hurry."

"No hurry, Cyril. Just not wasting time."

Cyril gives her an odd, speculative look, then decides to laugh.

"None of us getting any younger, eh?"

Hannah smiles, politely dismissing the remark, accepts the glass, and finally moves to the sofa.

"This is Christine," Edith explains as they all shift together to make space. "She's just moved into the Stephensons' house. You knew the Stephensons, didn't you? Well, I toddled across to say hullo and welcome and thought how nice it would be if we got together like this. Neighborly. Such a shame, I think, that leaving cards isn't done anymore. One slotted into a community so much more easily."

No applause is forthcoming. Hannah and Christine merely regard each other and Hannah says, "Hullo, Christine."

"What a beautiful dress," Christine says. "It's so subtle." She ends on a questioning note.

"Thank you," Hannah answers with none of the accompanying detail of source, inflated or reduced price, or requests for confirmation of taste that are normal in these circumstances. Edith sits crossly between them, unhappily suspecting that she may look like a Roman senator in her white silk. Christine is wearing a long skirt and a silk shirt, while

Janet has succeeded as always in making her own dress a safe blue anonymity.

"What part of the States are you from?" Edith tries again.

"California. I haven't been there for years, but the accent clings."

"Is your husband American too?" asks Janet, hoping he is. It would be exciting to have an American male in the neighborhood. She always thinks of Americans as males, so much more biological than men, who are British and safer, but not exciting, just inescapable.

"No, he's not. And by the way, he's not my husband. I mean, we're not married. We live together."

I shouldn't have got out of bed this morning, thinks Edith with desperation. The day was doomed from the start. I think I may be breaking down. Too much, too much to endure.

"Really?" she says aloud and hears with pleased surprise that she sounds unsurprised, sophisticated, and calm.

Janet turns red, then white. Living in sin. That means you like It. Only people who like It live together when they're not obliged to by society or clergy to have It. She eyes David voraciously. How does he do It? He must do wonderful, wicked things. A thrill runs through her as when she watches love scenes on TV or reads them in novels, a thrill unrelated to George or any part of her real life.

"Why?" says Hannah.

Oh my God, thinks Edith, she's going to do it again, but Christine is unperturbed.

"We're friends," she explains amiably. "You don't draw up contracts for friendship, do you, with lots of penalty clauses?"

Hannah nods, considering.

"You're against marriage then," Edith states, a patronizing I-know-better-than-you smirk on her lips.

"Not at all," Christine replies without heat. "I'm not against football, either, or tight corsets. They're just not for me."

Other women don't reprimand Edith, not even ever so delicately, but Christine seems oblivious. Effortlessly, safe in her envelope of detachment, she has the upper hand. The other three all recognize her for what she is: a free agent; if not free, the ties that tie her are of her own informed choice and making. Edith recognizes her with bitter envy, Janet with timorous awe, Hannah with excitement. It can be done. It really can.

"I'll see to the food," Edith says, rising. "Cyril, see to the seating, please."

She flows out of the room, her face hard, tired, and tears not far away.

Nine

They sit around the wreckage of Edith's dinner. All the preparation, the day's work spent on making it perfect, with everything polished and placed just so like a photograph for a glossy magazine, all, all reduced to a shambles. Wine spots on the cloth, crumbs of bread and cheese, flickers of ash on greasy plates, grape seeds and nutshells. The candlelight is generous to the heated faces and the last of the wine glows in clouded crystal. The whole is like a painting in oils, still, not quite three-dimensional, a composition of color dully highlighted and deeply shadowed.

It is late. Edith knows she must rise and shepherd everyone into the drawing room for coffee, otherwise the moment will be lost. The women will move into the drawing room for coffee and the men will start drinking port in here, and there will be no tidy leave-taking but a degeneration into reminiscence and bawdy laughter while the women's polite smiles become more and more acid, until the first bitter civilities turn into open hostility and one by one they take themselves off and away to their beds, grateful they are not required to perform and furiously wounded that they are not desired to perform.

"Come along, everyone," Edith says brightly. "Coffee in the other room."

No one wants to move. Janet smiles a glassy smile at Edith, Hannah holds her head high with an effort, Cyril ignores Edith and continues talking to Christine on his right.

Edith surveys the scene, all her guests sitting around her table, and wishes she were in bed. The meal has gone well, she supposes, but now it's time they all got up and went home. They have talked, there have been no sharp-edged silences, no sniping. Christine has described the way the lemons grow in California, compared climates and houses. David has done his share too. He has explained his function as a journalist, created questions for them all to ask so that everyone has been able to keep to the marked conversational path and avoid the dragons that lie in wait on either side.

"Come along," Edith repeats with resolute cheerfulness.

Hannah looks at her with some sympathy and touches Cyril's arm, interrupting him.

"Cyril, you've neglected me. Come and talk to me over coffee."

Christine, quick to respond, rises and calls to George, "We haven't had a chance to talk properly. I want to ask you about some places you mentioned."

Janet smiles all around, David gets up and holds out his hand to help her up. She's had more to drink than she should and is vague, but she sees a hand held out and clutches it.

"Good girl," says David, kind not patronizing.

Henry goes to Edith and says in a stage whisper with conventional gallantry, "I'll come and help you with the coffee. It seems the only way I can get you to myself."

Satisfied, Edith turns to go, with Henry, shrugging at Hannah, following.

Slowly the others drift into the drawing room and sit, sighing as if the meal has exhausted them, which it has. Cyril, moving slowly, pours brandy and port and Cointreau. No one speaks. Hannah lights a cigarette, then leans back in her chair and stares, absorbed, at the smoke rising and curling.

Janet sits sidesaddle on the edge of her chair, small and hunched, looking into her lap. Christine and David have taken seats beside each other. George lies back, his legs stretched out in front of him, his port loosely held on his middle. Edith and Henry come in, bringing the coffee, but they are slow and quiet and don't disturb the dream-ridden torpor. Edith pours, Henry takes the coffee around, then they sit.

Suddenly, Janet squeaks into the silence. "It would be wrong not to be married if you had children."

"What does 'wrong' mean?" David says lazily after a pause.

"What?" Janet.

"You have to define your terms." David again, not stern, not accusing, just factual. "Then we can be sure we're talking about the same thing."

Janet fidgets, frowns, twists her rings.

"Well . . . wrong's wrong, isn't it?" She looks around for agreement.

George snuffles into his port.

"Don't be so bloody silly, Jan," he says.

"That's unnecessary, George," Edith puts in sharply. "I know exactly what Janet means. Any right-minded woman does."

Cyril looks with disgust at Edith.

"Right-minded woman," he mimics, soprano. "What a load of codswallop. What the hell is it supposed to mean?"

Edith glares. Pores are breaking through her makeup, the enamel has cracked, and she is very tired.

"What a boor you are, Cyril," she hisses. "Drunk and coarse." Her eyes glitter as she speaks. "Don't make it more obvious than necessary that you're out of your depth." Cyril looks at each of the company in turn, making an appeal to the jury. Then he turns again to Edith.

"Out of my depth. Who pays, tell me that, you overblown cow, who pays? You? No, Madam. I pay, poor sod. My good self, your friendly neighborhood meal ticket."

Janet twitches in quiet anguish, knotted with uncomprehending embarrassment although this is a ritual she has witnessed often before. George is communing with his port and Henry is politely bored. Christine and David seem unperturbed and listen pleasantly as if Edith and Cyril were discussing holiday plans. Hannah is listening acutely with her newly tuned ears and is hearing the conversation differently from the way she has heard it a hundred times before. This is the way Edith and Cyril usually end an evening. It seems that alcohol acts as a kind of stripper, removing varnish and paint, burning through to the skin, and revealing the basic framework unadorned. Neither seems to remember it afterwards, it is as if it never happened, any comment from outside would be met with blank incomprehension, and then, next time, it happens again. And they both know all the naughty words. This Edith has always known all the words.

She leans toward Cyril.

"Listen, you bastard. I made you. I *made* you. You bought me because you knew you'd never make it without my background and my energy. And what did I get? Twenty-five years of propping up and pushing on and pretending not to notice the wandering eyes and the bottom-pinching. What did I get? An old, drunken lecher. An old, lecherous eunuch who thinks about it all the time and drools and doesn't do a bloody thing."

She tosses down her brandy and falls back exhausted.

Silence. Then Hannah says, clear and penetrating, "Why are we so unkind to each other? Wouldn't you have thought that we might have learned to be kind? We are all disappointed, at least I thought so." She nods at Christine and David. "Wouldn't it have been a small success to have learned to be kind?"

Silence again. Janet perks up and looks relieved.

"Huh," says Edith.

Cyril heaves himself to his feet and makes a tour refilling glasses before subsiding again into his chair.

"Go on," Christine prompts.

"That's all," Hannah says. "I see no need to qualify it. We are hideously unkind to each other, and we shouldn't be."

"Are you unkind?" asks David.

"Oh yes. I am too. But I would like to stop now. It takes so much energy. I am tired of trying to keep myself fluid enough to fit all the different molds people have of me and then blaming them because I am tired. It would be a relief to be myself and to be taken or left alone as that."

"Then be yourself."

"How can I know who is myself? How do I recognize someone I've never met? I thought yesterday that I knew, but things keep fluctuating and my certainty is eroded."

George looks sad.

"I know me," he says very softly, mourning. "But no one else does or wants to. No, you don't." He forestalls Janet who has opened her mouth to speak. "You least of all. You're the most fluid of any of us. It takes all your energy to the point where you have no shape, and I feel obliged to draw a more and more solid outline of this person I'm known as, to prevent the pair of us melting away altogether and running away down the drain like so much unset jelly."

"That's unkind," quivers Janet through trembling lips, horrified to find herself publicly discussed and yet nervously flattered at being a subject for comment.

"What's got into you, Hannah?" Cyril inquires. "You're behaving in a damned odd way lately."

"No, I'm not. I'm trying to be honest."

"Well that's not kind, for a start."

"Huh," says Edith again.

"Henry?" Cyril once more. "D'you think Hannah's being a bit odd? She's stirring it up a bit, wouldn't you say?" He squints at Henry.

Henry sips his port and thinks before he answers.

"Hannah," he says weightily, "this woman I live with, my wife, is a stranger. I don't know who she is."

"Oh, oh," says Janet.

David leans forward, listening, watching.

"There there, Janet," says Henry with sarcastic indulgence. "I know she said a naughty word. What is exercising me now is that so little a thing, one monosyllable in a particular context, has altered her position so entirely. So all right, the fact that she uttered it, though we all know that we all know the word, was a symptom. But for a whole society—a little one, true, but nevertheless a whole social structure—to be shaken

73

because one woman said one monosyllable when it wasn't considered suitable, well, it makes me think. And it wasn't a real word at that, nothing of the order of Death or Life or Love, but a footling expression of the uncleanness of loving."

This is unlike Henry. But he hasn't finished yet.

"Perhaps she's absolutely right. Our nice society is a house of cards and it's too bloody expensive. It costs too much in aggravation and in money, and the money, God help us, is the tangible manifestation of the hours and days and years of the time of our lives. We've paid with our lives. And for what?"

His voice rises, he's getting angry. At last he's passionate.

"For what? Nobody asked me if I wanted all of this rubbish. It's such a soft bloody sell you don't even notice you're being conned. All this bloody stupid made-in-Japan type of shoddy existence, and you pay with your life."

He's hurting now, he's feeling pain.

"It's not fair. It's not sodding fair. I want another go. Hannah's right. I want another bite at the cherry and this time, I'll be the one to decide what I pay."

He begins to subside. The others listen, but no one looks at him.

"I didn't ask to spend the hours of my days drilling dead, rotting tissue out of people's mouths and then filling up the holes with metals and plastics. I wanted to look at statues and pictures, pass days at a time absorbing one beautiful thing, make a lifetime's slow progress through Greece and Italy, looking and learning and feeling. So why didn't I? I know, and you all know. It isn't done, that's why. Look at me. Go on, look at me. I'm a success. Just like you, Cyril, and you, George. God help us all, we're successful men, so we can afford to fritter away what's left of life on drink and fantasies and, oh God help me, on garden gnomes."

In the booming silence that follows, Hannah wants to applaud. She's rather drunk by now, floating. If she closes her eyes, the invisible world swings smoothly and heavily around in her head. She can't decide whether that is less or more discomforting than keeping her eyes open and seeing these people, most of whom she accepts as full of rage and thwarted life as herself. She had thought herself the only one who suffered. Her own selfishness looms before her, but not as a blameworthy thing. She is tired out but she needs to be energetic now, to push herself and Henry because it would be so much easier just to float on without changing anything. It's going to take such energy, such force, to break the treadmill into such little pieces that it can't be cobbled together again, and her selfishness is the only tool that will crush hard enough. She's going to speak. She's not sure what she's going to say, but she's going to support Henry, but he sees her about to say something and turns on her furiously.

"Shut up," he shouts. "Shut up, shut up. You, you've said enough." He rises, spluttering, to his feet, pointing at Hannah, his glass of port slopping in his hand. "I was all right. I was unhappy, all right. But I was used to it, it was comfortable. There wasn't a way out so it was comfortable. I'd even forgotten that I wasn't Laughing Boy. Forgotten."

He runs suddenly out of steam and sits down again very deliberately.

"What's happening?" Janet asks, timid in the dreadful hush. "I don't understand."

No one else seems disposed to answer, so Hannah at last says soothingly, "It's all right, Janet. We've all had too much to drink. We should go home now."

"Yes. Oh yes." Janet gets to her feet in relief. "Come on, George. We must go home. Thanks for a lovely evening, Edith."

Edith stares at her. Cyril gets up and fetches her coat and puts it gently around her shoulders.

"Off you go then, Janet. George, come on, old man. Upsadaisy."

George looks up with beseeching eyes and encounters Janet's primly encouraging smile.

"Thank you for a lovely evening," he repeats in wonderment. "Thank you for a lovely evening, Edith. Thank you, Cyril, Henry, Hannah, for a lovely evening." He fumbles to his feet. "Lovely to meet you, Christine, David. Lovely. 'It's a lovely day tomorrow,'" he sings unexpectedly. "Come on, Janet, lovely Janet. Let's go home."

"Well, good night," Janet says politely to the room, and Cyril propels her and George to the door.

When he returns, no one has moved, and he goes around once more filling glasses before he sits.

"I thought," Hannah says pensively, beyond tiredness, "I thought it was going to be easy. I thought I'd banged all the problems in the world on the head, thwack. Thwack," she repeats, taking a gloomy enjoyment in the sound. "But it's not easy at all. I find I'm dreadfully confused now. It keeps coming and going. Now you see it, now you don't."

"See what?" It's David, coming in after many bars' rest. "What do you see?"

"I see that I had isolated my troubles, my pains. I felt myself all alone and separate and so they must be too, not touching anyone else. But I'm not an island after all, except inside my head. No, not even there. We all share the same pain, why can't we touch each other? I want . . . and Henry wants, but something, something forbids . . ."

She shakes her head and gives up.

"Try again," David presses, lightly relentless. "What do you want?"

She spreads her arms wide.

"Everything. My everything. I think we all have a different one. I want to see the lemons grow and hummingbirds and polar ice. I want to be rapturously happy and run like a girl toward . . . I don't know."

"And the other side? What about pain, rejection, hunger? Have you known them? Have you always been happy, even if only a little bit? Safe, comfortable?"

Hannah looks at him. "I don't know even that. With what should I compare my life? I have no standard of comparison to know whether I've been more or less than anything. No, I don't think I've known what is usually meant by pain, or hunger. My condition has been chronic, never acute." She looks anxiously from David to Christine and back again and then, sighing, at Henry. "It's time to go. Edith's asleep, I think. Shall I see you again?"

"Come any time," Christine says, her firm, quiet voice suddenly establishing solidity in the quicksand of the disarranged room.

"Yes. Yes, I will," Hannah says, rising. The others all rise too. Poor Cyril, poor tired Cyril, left with the bills and the clearing up, wearily goes and fetches coats.

"I don't know what you're all talking about," he mutters. "I'm getting too old for this late-night philosophizing. You'd better see the quack and let him give you some happy-pills, Hannah. You're being damned odd."

"Yes, I know, Cyril," Hannah says kindly, pecking his cheek. "I'm sorry it turned so sour this evening. Go to bed now. I'll come and help Edith clear in the morning."

Henry, morose and stubbornly monosyllabic, says a curt good night and they leave together, he and Hannah and David and Christine, leaving Cyril to the salvaging of Edith.

The Jacksons reach their door in silence.

"You thought it was going to be easy," Henry erupts without warning, halfway up the stairs. "That's all I've heard. I, I, I."

Hannah begins to cry, not loudly, just a streaming of tears down her stale makeup.

"I thought we'd understood each other. We talked. We did talk, Henry."

"You talked. You bloody talked. You chucked your bombshell and then you talked. My God, you talked. *I'll* talk in the morning. I'm going to bed."

He turns his back on her and goes to their bedroom, leaving her dazed, horrified. She can't appraise the situation now. She's too deadly tired. She goes to bed and very quickly and quietly cries herself to sleep.

Ten

Friday. Hannah wakes to find that Henry has already left the bed. Her mouth feels foul after too much to drink and too many cigarettes. Her chest aches and she almost smiles at the flash of anxiety it causes her and at the conditioned reaction, "I must give up smoking." Her ankles hurt and when she stands she feels fat and heavy and her stomach sticks out almost pregnantly. She puts on her new dressing gown, a flowing wine-red robe, and finds that it makes her look dreadfully ill, draining all color from her face. She defies the bedroom mirror: What the hell. I feel like death, why not look like it?

She is gloomy this morning, but not entirely because of the disturbances in her mind. The day is gray, the garden beyond the window looks defeated, and Hannah has an awareness of the disaster-area of Edith's dining room lying in wait for her. It's masochistic to get up and embark on such a morning. If she gets back into bed and closes her eyes, it might just go away without noticing her and dragging her with it. She sighs, wishes last night had not happened, and goes along the landing to the stairs, arranging her face and feelings. So Henry's confused, he doesn't know if he's coming or going, he feels he's not in control of events. Quite right too. He's not. Hannah is. Well, not exactly, not what you could call in control, but she's in there fighting, and she's got a hand on the wheel and she's not letting go.

This "simplicity" as she had so naïvely conceived it has turned into a kind of tug-of-war. First one side looks overwhelmingly likely to win, then suddenly they all fall down on their bottoms and the other side makes ground again and it's an equal pull with no advantage to either side, just an eye-bulging struggle to stay in the same place.

"It isn't fair," thinks Hannah childishly, stopping halfway down the stairs and sitting there to consider. "Opponents are supposed to be evenly matched, weight for weight. Henry's heavier than me, he has all the advantage of custom and experience and confidence. I'm the Red Queen in *Alice,* running like mad to stay in the same place while the world whips away under my feet. I need progress. I caught him on the hop the other evening, gained a tiny bit of ground, and thought I'd won the war. Pathetic. I don't even know who I'm fighting anymore. It could be me as much as him."

Henry comes out of the kitchen into the hallway and looks up the stairs. He looks terrible. He hasn't shaved, his eyes are bloodshot, and his hair is a threadbare tousle. He regards Hannah in silence. She studies him in return.

"You look awful, Henry. Do you feel very ill?"

"What are you doing sitting on the stairs wearing that thing at this time of the morning?"

"What time is it?"

"Getting on for eight."

"Oh. You'll be late if you don't hurry." She knows Henry is constitutionally incapable of hurry. He always has to leave himself plenty of time for things so that he doesn't have to rush. Rushing is inefficient, he says, and leads to mistakes which will later take more time to rectify. He has explained it to her countless times. "This is my new dressing gown," she mentions unnecessarily.

"It looks ridiculous. Are you going up or coming down? I want to shave."

"Oh Henry," she says, leaning forward and holding out her hands, "can't we at least keep each other company a little bit?"

79

Henry starts up the stairs, brushing roughly past her.

"Don't start all that again. I'm sick of all this instant philosophy. A load of sick rubbish. There's no need for any of it. Talking arty-crafty nonsense off the top of your head. You know perfectly well you will have the operation. You'll have it done privately on the insurance and then we can have an end to all this dramatizing and get back to normal."

He slams the bathroom door behind him.

Hannah sits open-mouthed on the stairs. It's Henry back the way he was three days ago, three years ago, bossiness firing on all cylinders. She's gained no ground at all, whatever she thought. What now? Quiet little Hannah, should she creep down the rest of the stairs without further comment, but bursting with resentment, or will the updated Hannah come and give her a hand? Not will she, but can she?

Hannah pulls her robe into a bundle in front of her and goes down the stairs without a word. In the kitchen she turns on the grill, slaps bacon on it, breaks an egg viciously into a frying pan, posts slices of bread into the toaster, measures coffee into the pot, fuming to herself.

One of these days. One of these days, I'll give him such a telling, he won't know what hit him. He'll be sorry. Oh, I'll make him sorry.

She deals plates on to the table, crashes through the cutlery drawer, furiously, impotently angry. I wish I had a dog. I'd kick it. I'd kick its teeth in. I'd tear it apart.

She slams around the kitchen, panting, her teeth so tightly clenched they hurt, tears of rage blurring her vision.

How dare he? How *dare* he? Treating me like some idiot girl. *Telling* me, *ordering* me. Who does he think he is? What does he think I am?

The table is laid, the breakfast organized. She glares at it all until hearing the bathroom door open and Henry coming down the stairs, then habit asserts itself and she instantly smooths her face into a neutral expression, mops her eyes with the front of her robe, and turns to the sink, pretending to be busy with taps as he comes in. He says nothing, not even his customary "Right," but scrapes his chair back and sits.

"Coffee?" he inquires coldly.

Hannah grips the edge of the sink tightly, feeling the spasm of anger threatening to overtake her again. "Coffee?" just like that. She looks down at her knuckles, white against the white of the sink, and her robe, wine-red. Not a beautiful blue. Red. Ridiculous, is it? She forms the anger into a neat ball and swallows it.

"Did you say something, Henry?" she asks sweetly.

"My coffee has not been poured," he points out sternly.

Aha, she thinks. I'm being put in my place. You've got to keep these women down, right, Henry, old pal? Otherwise they get above themselves and think they're as good as you.

"Yassuh, Massa, Boss," she says aloud, lifting the coffee pot. "Coffee you want, coffee you shall have. I'm only sorry I haven't got any Turkish Delight to offer you. Would you like me to grovel now or later when you're not in a hurry?"

Henry stops chewing.

"What?" He looks so bewildered she giggles.

"I said, oh mighty caliph, pour your own sodding coffee."

She bangs the pot down on the table so hard that his plate jumps, and Henry jumps and Hannah laughs despite herself. "You're a bully, Henry Jackson. And a coward. You let me believe you cared enough at least to listen to me with some respect, but now you're afraid so you start your old bullying again. Don't you give me orders, Henry, or I'll smack your hand."

"You're out of your mind," he gasps, swallowing an inconvenient mouthful of egg and bacon.

"Don't you wish I were," she divines accurately. "Think how easy that would be for you. Lots of sympathy and credit, and no Hannah cramping your style, and no guilt feelings about forcing operations either. You'd be having your cake *and* eating it."

He starts to bluster, making a clumsy effort to placate her though now she is the one who is calm.

"Now Hannah, you're not well. I spoke to the doctor. He confirmed all you said. You really have got . . . it."

She nods, smiling approval.

"Well done, Henry, old pal. Don't take Hannah's word for it. Check up on her. She's out of her mind, you know."

"It's your condition. You're in a very turbulent state. Shock . . ."

"Aw shut up," she says as coarsely as she can manage and gets up. "I'm going away, Henry. I'm going to get myself together. I'm going away."

"I'll be late. I must be off," he says hurriedly, leaving the table and rinsing his hands at the sink.

"You heard me. Pretend you didn't if you like. But you know what I said, and you know I know you know." She giggles again. "Well, you know what I mean. 'Bye, Henry. Have a nice day."

She whisks out of the kitchen and up the stairs, feeling mean but victorious. It's not an unpleasant feeling. Perhaps that's why Henry always has to win an argument, because it gives him a nice feeling? Poor old Henry. Yesterday she loved him. A few days earlier she was full of anger and dislike of him. Today, well, today she doesn't seem to care much just at the moment, but moments are coming and going at such a rate lately, there's no telling what may develop. She trips over the red robe at the top of the stairs and realizes she is still not entirely sober.

"Whoops. I'll have a bath and think about things," she tells herself aloud, and Henry, still standing, gaping, in the kitchen, says, "What? Hannah."

" 'Bye Henry," she calls dismissively over the banister and locks herself into the bathroom. There is silence downstairs for a minute, then she hears the front door close and the car start and drive away. It's very quiet afterwards. Very quiet. Hannah listens to the quiet, leaning against the locked door. It carries an echo of Henry's rebuking voice and of her own killing flippancy, aimed with precision at the heart of his authority. It presses in close against her, clammy and menacing.

"What have I done?" she whispers fearfully. "What have I done?"

She sits on the edge of the bath and is filled with fear. "Oh my God, I've got what I asked for. What did Mother say . . . ? 'Be careful what you wish for, my girl. You may get it.' I've sent him too far away ever to come back now."

She perches on the side of the bath for a long time, shaking. The shaking starts with her hands and spreads through her until she is shaking uncontrollably from her head to her feet. Her teeth are chattering and she is very much afraid.

Without Henry, really, actually, without him, how will she manage? She's never had a chance to find out whether she is able to be alone. She has never, never been alone.

"Oh damn, damn, damn," she mutters. "How much more can there be that I don't know? There isn't any independent me. I really don't exist apart from him. No one believes in me except as part of the package."

Still shivering violently, she turns on the hot tap, filling the room with steam, trying to warm herself. Her feet are so cold they don't register the heat of the water as she steps in, and she nearly scalds herself. It was only a few minutes ago. Surely it can unhappen. Please, God, make it unhappen. Go on, God, you can do it if you want to. I'm not ready yet. But God isn't listening, or else He has listened and answered her and she has overlooked the cold truth that *no* is as much of an answer as *yes*.

Gradually, as she lies in the hot water, the trembling stops. Hannah lies still, feeling very tired, trying to empty her mind, which won't let itself be emptied but slowly settles into a quietness of sorts.

David suggested last night that her longings were based on incomplete foundations, that she has had too much ease, no acquaintance with harsh realities. Some he specified, and it's true she has no experience of hunger or poverty or crippling grief, and she herself had already put passion on the list. Now she adds being alone. It's the only one she can do anything about. The others can't be manufactured, conjured out of circumstances. To be alone, successfully, would be to accomplish something before the crab runs riot. What does "successfully" mean? She doesn't know yet, but if she tries it, surely she will recognize success or failure. It's obvious. She didn't mean it when she said it to Henry, not really, it was just something to say, to blight his breakfast, but it's what she must do. Go away, be on her own, and find out whether or not she is capable of self-sufficiency.

If she's not, if it happens that she crumbles into demands and admissions of dependence, she will at least then be able to accept her weakness as a proven fact and take a little comfort from knowing that she had found enough strength to seek the proof.

She begins to feel better, encouraged, stimulated even. She must go to Edith's, having promised, but after that there are plans to be made, possibilities to comb through. She determines to reach the night with a decision made. As she dresses, putting on, without considering it as significant or insignificant, clothes that were a part of the former Hannah, she realizes that it doesn't matter anymore about making declarations with such trivial things as her clothes, since she is ready now to make declarations with her whole life. They were a necessary first step, and she enjoys them, and the new hair and face, and everything, but they were only the beginning, a little starter. The main course comes next and that's going to be the pièce de résistance. She spares a moment to wonder wryly how the pudding will turn out, but turns her mind resolutely from the thought as it brings an icy lurch to her stomach. She must not let herself think about it.

Ought she to phone Henry and say sorry? She finds herself hovering over the telephone before leaving the house and tuts impatiently at herself. There is no other person in the world Henry would address with such rudeness, and he has to stop thinking he need not treat her with the same care he would any other person. But still she has her hand on the phone and is getting annoyed at her indecision. This is getting really boring, not knowing from one moment to the next how she feels about Henry. It would be such a help to feel one way or another conclusively. The quiet, suppressed resentment of years was at least predictable. One had a framework in which to function. Hannah looks back on her familiar, aching discontent with something not far from nostalgia.

She sighs hugely.

"Oh hell. What a mess." There's no simplicity left. It's like going for a driving lesson in a mini and finding in the middle of the rush hour traffic that it's turned into a thirty-ton truck. There's no going back now. She's done and said too much. There's not a hope of going back. Irrevocable changes have taken place, so even if she buckled under and said, "Yes, Henry, no, Henry, whatever you say, Henry," nothing can be retrieved. So, she concludes dryly, giving the phone a farewell pat and turning her back on it, it appears she's in the truck-driving business.

She sets off toward Edith's, resolved to stop swaying this way and that, making, unmaking, and remaking up her mind. About two years, give or take a little. Minus three days already. All of her days could so easily be dissipated by indecision until they're used up, gone, with nothing achieved, nothing stated, only herself and Henry torn to rags to no purpose. An ignoble end to an almost noble enterprise. That would really be a most culpable waste and would leave a nasty mess afterwards. She walks on, looking at her feet in their good leather lace-up shoes. One two, one two, they go. Her feet, alive and walking. Soon she'll have no need for shoes. Her feet will be gray-white, with obscene toenails, bloodless, dead, the animating spirit gone.

Where?

A shock of fear hits her, so violent that bitter fluid rushes into her mouth and she stumbles and nearly falls. From one instant to the next, the finality, the reality, the shortness of her time change from barely recognized projection to concrete, inescapable fact.

Gasping for breath, with cold sweat on her forehead, she begins to walk again, feverishly ticking off things she will do today. Talk to Edith . . . she has lots of contacts, might she not have ideas of places to go? She may have to tell Edith, but that can be decided when the state of Edith today has been assessed.

Phone the boys. They must know now. They must understand her purpose if they can, and they never will if all they hear is the Gospel according to Henry, or nothing at all.

Money. Questions about money present themselves. She will need some money, and Henry has always played his money cards very close to his chest, been downright secretive in fact. Hannah must go and see the bank manager and insist on answers. Lots to do. A busy day. Fill it up, leaving no cracks for panic to slip in through. First Edith's clearing up. It shouldn't take very long, then she can get on.

A tiny trickle of blood, or something, makes itself felt, and Hannah runs the last yards to Edith's door, runs not to try to get away from it, scuttling crab, chasing her, but just to outstrip it, to show it that it has to wait, that it isn't nightfall yet and she has things to do.

Eleven

Edith opens the door ready to repel salesmen. She has done her best, using a lot of colors, to disguise the effects of last night, and the first impression is of a technicolor-movie queen. Then the dispirited falling away of skin from prominent facial bones emerges, and the tiny lines vertically along her upper lip, and the darkened skin of her neck.

Her haughty expression is at once discarded when she sees that it is Hannah standing there, very pale and with wide, wondering eyes.

Funny, thinks Edith without noticing she's thinking it, I always thought Hannah had rather small eyes. Not noticeable at all.

"Oh hullo," she says coolly. "It's you. It's all right, you know. You needn't have bothered. But come in now you're here."

Hannah steps into the hall and closes the door behind her, as Edith has immediately walked away toward the kitchen, calling over her shoulder, "I got everything done in very short order this morning. I was rather tired last night, that's all. There's hardly anything left to do."

Hannah comes into the kitchen and stands in the doorway, playing nervously with her scarf.

Edith says, "I suppose you'd like some coffee," and sets about making it. Hannah remains silent. She's looking at her hands fidgeting with the scarf, and they're saying to her: We'll be dead soon, along with all the rest of you. Dead. Lying in a hole in the ground. Left out to rot in all weathers until we fall into putrefaction. How will you like that, then? She stares at Edith's back, incapable of speech, until an appalling mewling sound comes from her mouth. Edith turns, startled, and Hannah's mouth gapes at her and Hannah's eyes come toward her and Hannah's hands clutch clawlike at the air.

Edith drops the cup she's holding and it breaks noisily on the floor.

Hannah begins to breathe again, taking in a long noisy breath. As if on wooden legs, she moves in jerks to a chair and very carefully sits down, gasping.

Neither speaks. Edith pushes the shards of the cup away with her foot and sits across the table from Hannah, white and frightened herself so that the paint on her face stands out hideously, her hands shaking so that she must clasp them together and keep her eyes on them. Hannah and Edith remain thus for several seconds, a long time, until the blessed ordinariness of a kitchen on a Friday morning in early spring establishes itself around Hannah again, and she feels humanity return to fill the well of cornered animal in her. She takes a deep breath and brushes her hand across her cold forehead.

Edith raises her eyes and sees that it is Hannah sitting there, not a monster that goes around frightening good women in their kitchens. They both start to speak at once and stop.

Then Hannah says, "It's terrible. I'm sorry."

And Edith says, "God, you frightened me."

She rises, leaning heavily on the table, goes out to the drawing room, and returns with a bottle of brandy.

"I think we'd be justified in dosing ourselves a little," she says briefly, fetching two glasses and pouring a generous measure into each. "Obviously there's something very wrong."

She waits. Hannah looks about her, fixing her eyes on each

kitchen appliance in turn, anchoring herself in time and normality with the cooker and the fridge and the washing machine, terrified of looking at any part of her own body in case it should wither and decay as she watches. She wants to speak, she wants to cry, but she is compelled to sit still, holding herself tightly together, resisting all movement in case she should start disintegrating and leave Edith sitting drinking brandy with a skeleton.

Edith pushes a glass of brandy toward her, and Hannah, with immense concentration, contrives to lock her fingers around it and bring it to her lips. Her teeth clatter against the rim and some of the brandy trickles down her chin before she manages to swallow. The flame of it makes her shudder, then relax, leaning back in her chair and giving a great sigh. Unexpectedly, Edith leans across and tenderly wipes Hannah's chin with her fingertips. Her fingers are warm and soft and alive and Hannah, surprised by such a gentle gesture from Edith, begins at last to cry.

She cries for a long time, sitting up in the kitchen chair, her hands lying on the tabletop like an obedient child's, and Edith waits patiently, her hand on Hannah's, looking out through the kitchen window as if she were wondering what to cook for lunch. Hannah cries undramatically, with an even rhythm like a steady fall of summer rain.

After a time, when Hannah's weeping starts abating, Edith removes her hand, pats Hannah's briskly, and says, "Time to stop now. Do you want to tell me?"

Hannah mops her eyes, blows her nose, and straightens her shoulders.

"I didn't. I've been peculiar, I know, like Cyril said, and probably offended you very much, but I think I have to tell you. I have no friend to turn to, you see."

The admission of that, which she has always known but falsely dismissed as unimportant with a see-if-I-care toss of her head, renews her tears, but she gulps them down and pushes her face back into position with her hands.

Edith nods sadly, not denying the failure of friendship. It's the same for her. Friendship so easily equals dependence and Edith's whole being is based on superiority through independence.

"It hasn't meant a great deal till now," Hannah continues. "I've thought it would be nice to have someone I could tell anything to, perhaps cry with from time to time. You know, someone you could tell your sins to, or phone in the middle of the night, and know they'd still love you, no matter what. But I've never met anyone . . ."

"I know," Edith says, and she and Hannah look at each other directly, for this once at least on equal terms.

"I've got cancer. I'm going to die."

Edith's eyes grow wide, but she makes no move and doesn't speak for several seconds.

"Do you have to? There are cures."

"Oh Edith. Could you possibly understand?" First the doctor, then Henry, now Edith. Hannah is desperate at the thought of going through it all again, but the need for someone, anyone, to understand is overpowering.

"I could have an operation, but I don't want to. I feel that this is the way it's meant to be. You don't have to tell me it's not a reasonable feeling, I know that, but it's a real feeling. I've denied my feelings, subjugated them to reason, for so long, and I want simply to let whatever is going to happen happen without trying to contort it into a 'reasonable' shape. I want fate or God or whatever it's called to have a free hand for once, and I want not to argue or fight but just accept my place in time, and for everyone to accept my right to choose that."

She takes another sip of brandy, and her voice is getting steadier, becoming almost authoritative.

"It's my right. It's anybody's right. If you say how you want your body disposed of after death, your request is honored strictly, unless you ask for something positively harmful to other people. But everyone says you're mad, or criminal, if you try to dispose of your living body and mind to suit yourself."

"Henry. Naturally."

"Well, yes. Naturally. Except that Henry doesn't want to live the rest of his life with me, and I'm tired of mine. You heard what he said. There's nothing, nothing to stop him doing what he says he wants to, except the social mental block. He can't because he's married, albeit unrewardingly, and he's got his dental practice and his house and his clubs and his reputation, the whole works. But it's he himself, because of his heredity, that lets those things be reason enough for crushing the life out of him and not making any attempt to change the pattern. If I weren't there, that would break the Chinese puzzle and release him. He won't contemplate it otherwise. He's pinned to the ground. At first he reacted instinctively and seemed to see what I meant, but then all the social thumbscrews tightened again and he's torn by guilt twice over. Once because he's sure he has to force me to conform, and once because he doesn't want to."

"I see," says Edith. Hannah doesn't know whether she means she really does see or whether it's just words, but then Edith goes on.

"It gives some sort of meaning to last night's conversation, for a start. It was pretty obscure at the time." She looks thoughtfully into her glass. "What are you, anyway, Hannah? A fool or a saint? You want to die so Henry can have his little plaster gnomes?"

Hannah's mouth twists bitterly. She should have known better. This is Edith, remember? Edith who does things her way and makes everyone conform. Edith who with impunity calls her husband names. What can she know of prison, of failure or hopelessness?

"I mean," Edith continues, "I quite see that life with Henry could be stultifying . . . no offense, I like him, but then I haven't lived with him year in year out . . . but isn't it a bit extreme to die? It's permanent, you know. Oh, I've wanted to die, more times than I can tell you, but only for a little while, until Cyril's really hurting, not forever."

Hannah stares at her. What could Cyril, bumbling, kind Cyril with his round tummy and his unconvinced and unconvincing passes, possibly do to make Edith want to die? In

Hannah's experience, it takes a quantity of alcohol in conjunction with provocation from Edith to produce any spark in him at all. She shakes her head in disbelief and Edith smiles wryly.

"Yes, I know," she says. "Good old Cyril. Everybody's friend. I'll tell you something I've kept to myself for a hell of a long time."

She pauses. It's clearly very hard to say. She looks up and laughs suddenly.

"I loved him. How about that?"

Her mouth twists in a grimace that's an attempt at a smile. Hannah says nothing, not knowing what to say, not sure Edith wants her to answer.

"Funny, isn't it? You fall in love . . . oh you do," she disputes Hannah's doubt, "and you love him so much that you understand why the sun rises in the morning. It's just to shine on him. You can't believe that he actually chooses you when there are all those other girls with so much more going for them. But he says he loves you. He even believes himself that he loves you. He seeks you out, can't keep away from you, swears he'll never hurt you, and all the time you suspect that what he means by love is only skin-deep and yours is built into the very tissue of your life. But you say to yourself, why not take what you can while you've got the chance? Glory in it and pay later. The thing is, you've no means of knowing in advance what the price is or whether you'll be able to pay. So you're afraid. Scared to your soul of the time coming when he's going to realize what he's done and doesn't want you anymore."

Edith starts to cry, tears running gently down her face, but her voice is steady.

"So you build up your defenses. You have to get ready to pretend you don't care particularly when the moment comes so that you can survive. You get so sensitive to every word he says, listening for the words he isn't saying, and being so bloody careful what you say that you constantly say the wrong thing and make him angry. You get tied up in knots. And as he cools, he begins to believe your pretense and starts feeling you're an encumbrance, and you start trying to unbuild your defenses and show him how much you care, but you can't because now he's moving away from you and you need them more than ever, and the knots get tighter and tighter and he moves farther and farther away and the day comes when he shows you, beyond doubt, that you're not the star of the show any longer, but a pitiful extra he can't easily get rid of. That's when you want to die. Because he's your life, and without him you're dead already. And then, from somewhere in the long nights you find a shred of anger to cover your nakedness with and you want to live, if for no better reason then to punish him.

"Me and Cyril. Me holding on because he's mine, hating him because he promised never to hurt me and I can't forgive him for hurting me to the point where I thought no one could be so hurt and still move and breathe. And him hating me for putting the chains on him and for making him feel guilty that his love wasn't what he said it was, so he'd better pay up and shut up. Our lives are corroded and there's no way out."

The tears are pouring down Edith's face now. She has shrunk in her chair, she is small and piteous, not in the least recognizable as the armored Edith of the coffee-mornings. Hannah has forgotten her own anguish.

Edith speaks again, painfully, her throat hurting. "If I could have clung a bit, made him see how much I needed him to love me, perhaps it would have been different. But I couldn't let myself. I knew almost from the beginning that it was too marvelous to last and I had to prepare myself, otherwise I'd have looked like an idiot. And being left with egg on my face was the one thing I never could tolerate."

"Poor Edith," says Hannah gently, and Edith doesn't mind because it's not said with offensive pity, no trace of egg in it. "If I had known, I would have been different toward you."

"Yes, I know," Edith says, mopping her face and struggling to put it together again. "I've always been specially overbearing with you because I saw you being the sort of wife who could probably have held Cyril, and I was jealous that you could do it and I couldn't."

"But I didn't want to be like I was," Hannah cries sharply. This is too dreadful to endure, so many anguishes. "I've been suffocated. Henry's done my living for me. I have no will, no existence. I want to get out."

She is getting shrill.

"Edith, I can't die without living first, even for a little while. I don't even have real memories like you. No passions, no griefs, no past. I've got to come into focus."

Edith gives a great sigh and shakes her head, agreeing, despairing.

"Then you'll have done something independently of Henry and got your own way and pushed Henry into a position where he can't blame anyone but himself for the misuse of his opportunities. Yes. I understand."

"Thank God," says Hannah.

Edith smiles faintly at her and they sit quietly until Edith says, "I must go and see to my face. I'm a mess. Put the kettle on, will you?"

She hurries out of the kitchen and by the time Hannah has made fresh coffee she's back with her paint touched up and looking very nearly the usual Edith.

Hannah has to ask, "Edith? Doesn't it get any easier as time goes by? I mean, do you still love him?"

Edith fusses with cups and saucers, rattles spoons.

"Oh I don't know," she says in her best, brittle coffee-morning voice. "I've forgotten."

Hannah bows her head, rebuked. Edith and Hannah again, nearly.

"Right," Edith says crisply. "What's to be done? You have considered other possibilities . . . the operation, then a separation?"

"I really don't want to make such an effort. I'd still have this sense of borrowed time. I never was a borrower, was I? Always too nervous to use a borrowed thing. I want to go away, by myself, to see how I get on alone."

"How long?"

"Altogether? About two years, but that's very approximate."

"Are you very frightened?"

"Very. Very very at times, like this morning. Not of dying. Of being dead." She shivers as the ice jumps inside her again.

"Can you live alone, being afraid?"

"I don't know. I want to try. If I can I'll have some respect for myself. There's a niggle in my mind that I'm just being hysterical. I want to get rid of that."

"Well . . . there's our cottage in Suffolk. It's got a spare room and we're seldom there. Even when we are, the spare room's quite independent. We did it up as a flat for Sarah when she wanted to play at being a bachelor girl."

Sarah is Edith's grown-up daughter.

Hannah looks up, eager and anxious.

"You're welcome to it, if you want it. It would be a base till you decide on something."

"What about Cyril?"

"Cyril needn't be involved. He doesn't like it anyway. It's been for sale for months, but there haven't been any takers. If anyone comes, you could show them around."

"Thank you, Edith. I wish we had known each other better."

Edith looks thoughtful.

"I wonder if we would have liked each other better. Probably not. I've always been impatient with good little women like you. Though without you there'd be no one for women like me to bully."

Hannah laughs a little. So does Edith, and they are laughing when there's a tap at the back door.

"Who on earth can that be?" asks Edith, getting up to answer. "No one ever comes around to the back."

It is David Howard.

"Good heavens, David," Edith exclaims. "Come in. This is a surprise."

"I've come to offer my services as washer-up, and in search of information," says David.

"Oh, hullo, Hannah." If he's surprised to see her there, he doesn't show it.

Hannah wishes she'd repaired her face as Edith had, but it's too late. She mumbles a greeting and half rises.

"Don't go," says Edith, a shade too quickly. He's an unknown quantity, this unmarried man. "Coffee, David? We were just having some. If I'm going to have to be intelligent, I'll need some more."

"Great. Well, Hannah, how are you this morning?"

He asks as if it's a genuine question, requiring an answer. It flusters Hannah. Everything he says means something, and she's not used to that, accustomed to a society where conversation is rigorously kept on the surface of thought. Last night was an exception precipitated by Hannah herself and by the presence of David.

"Fine," she says with a bright smile.

He raises his eyebrows and gives her an interrogatory look. They all sit around the table and Edith and Hannah pay exaggerated attention to their coffee.

David says, "I expect you're wondering why I called this meeting," and Edith and Hannah laugh too merrily.

"Well . . ." Edith breaks the deadlock by deciding to chair the meeting. "What can I do for you, David?"

"I'm doing a series of articles on small stately homes for an American magazine. There's a widespread idea, you know, that all British people either live in castles and have tea with the Queen once a week or else live in hovels along with their livestock and tug their forelocks at the gentry. I'm filling in the gaps. Now I'm told East Anglia is particularly full of the kind of house I have in mind, and Cyril mentioned that you have connections there."

"Well, yes. I don't know about the whole of East Anglia. I was born in Essex, and we have a cottage in Suffolk, but I'm afraid there's very little I can tell you about stately homes. I should think you'd have to go and see."

"There isn't one in your village, wherever your cottage is? One you know something about, its place in the community. I'd like to find some personal stories of the minor gentry's influence on communities through the centuries. You know, 'My great-grandfather and the squire were churchwardens together' kind of thing."

"It sounds fascinating," Hannah says. "What a happy thing to do."

"Happy? That's an unusual choice of word."

Hannah is at once shy again.

"I meant," she explains rather crossly, "it sounds a delightful way of making a living."

"Perhaps Hannah could do some groundwork for you," Edith puts in. Hannah gapes at her, shocked. David is interested.

"She's going to spend some time at the cottage in Suffolk," Edith goes on smoothly. "Aren't you, Hannah?"

"Well, I don't know for sure . . . I might . . . it's not decided . . ."

"Of course it is," Edith says, fixing her eyes on Hannah. "It's quite decided. There's no time to change decisions."

Hannah is confused. She's being rushed, Edith has taken over. But Edith is only implementing Hannah's wishes. Only it's one thing to wish for something broadly and from a place of safety and another to find your wish suddenly operational and taking off, taking you with it willy-nilly.

"I'd be glad of some help."

"Won't Christine be helping you?" asks Hannah, playing for time.

"Why?" David's answer first stops her, then provokes her.

"Why not?" she demands, irritated. "Why this, why that? You really do tear things to bits, don't you?"

"Yes," he agrees complacently. "People get annoyed and then they speak without thinking and say what they really mean."

"I don't choose to speak without thinking," Hannah snaps. "I will say what I choose to say and then I'll know where I am. It's important that I know where I am."

Edith looks from one to the other, sensing that there's an exchange going on that isn't what it seems. Hannah doesn't understand. She merely knows that she has inadvertently lowered her guard and has been pulled onto quicksand again.

"That's settled then," David says.

"What?"

"You'll be in Suffolk, and you'll do a bit of asking and a bit of listening for me. Nothing time-consuming."

"Why not?" purrs Edith. "It would be interesting."

Hannah feels like a puppet again. . . . Pull this string and her head will jerk. Pull that string and her arm will wave. Her head nods.

"Good." David and Edith smile.

"Well, good-bye," Hannah breaks curtly into the approving silence. "I must go." She gets up and David rises too.

"It's arranged then?" Edith looks up with a trace of anxiety in her face and her voice. "It's all settled?"

Hannah looks at her hands, quiescent now, then at Edith, who has suffered and survived and is still suffering and surviving and will go on suffering and surviving because no date has been fixed for her execution and she will not conveniently lie down and die. Edith wants her to take a stand, to survive too, even if for so short a time. Edith wants the lonely two of them, Hannah and Edith, to bear each other company. So she's being pushy and Hannah resents it.

"What's the point?" she asks finally, tiredly, ignoring David.

"I don't know. To finish what one starts, perhaps. Integrity."

David has faded from their awareness. Edith and Hannah are alone again.

"I wouldn't have done it your way," Hannah says.

"Nor I yours. But the decisions really weren't ours."

"No."

Hannah has teetered on the brink long enough. She has talked and argued beyond the point of no return.

"I've got to go, haven't I?" Still she seeks confirmation.

"I think so."

She picks up her scarf, pulls her coat around her, and goes to the door.

"I'll see you then," David says. "I'll see you soon."

"If you like." Hannah has lost interest in him. "Good-bye, Edith."

Twelve

Now, two weeks later, here is Hannah in Suffolk. In Edith's cottage. Alone.

She's sitting in the living room on the edge of a chair, her knees together, her hands clutching her handbag on her lap, leaning forward, as if she were waiting for a train. Her aloneness is all around her like luggage. She doesn't know what to do with it.

The unfamiliar walls and furniture don't want to know her. She's only passing through so it's not worth their while to offer friendship. A small rain is falling outside onto a street that doesn't know Hannah and has nothing to do with her. All the films she's ever seen about travelers caught in transit between life and death come into her mind. She's seen them on ships, on planes, in trains, in hotels, even in country cottages like this, dead but not disposed of, waiting to be directed to one place or the other. So she sits waiting, unable to acknowledge that no one is going to come and nothing is going to happen unless she instigates it.

Henry drove her down. He was very strained and cross. Henry is still feeling that there is time, just, to indulge Hannah in her neurotic fantasy, before, for her own good, he takes matters into his own hands and if necessary carries her by force to the operating table. It's difficult, though, because being indulgent doesn't come easily to Henry. It's alien to his nature and he's profoundly impatient with the fantasy that Hannah is forcing on him. He has been alarmed into indulgence by the strength of her determination and the revelations it has brought, but it strains the equilibrium almost to the breaking point. His desire is to put an end to all this messing about, to present Hannah with arrangements readymade, to have her opened up, sewed up, and to resume as nearly as possible their humdrum, hopeless, socially acceptable normalcy. Most of all, he blames Hannah for the breach she made in the wall of his fortress, letting in a shaft of Grecian light that danced over the sullen interior and made him remember that the world is still out there. That was cruel. Tantalizing him with a glimpse of his heart's desire when he had almost forgotten what it was and had quite given up hoping for it. So he treats her very warily, speaking only when he has prepared complete sentences, withdrawing remarks the moment he's uttered them, feeling she's a bomb that could go off any second and he doesn't know what will trigger it. Very upsetting. Very unnatural, treading, speaking, breathing with nerve-stretching caution, not daring to fall asleep.

Hannah has been tender with Henry too. She is overawed that she has actually given utterance to the silent tirades of twenty years, she is breathlessly elated by her daring, sickeningly afraid of having burned her boats when she can't be sure she won't need them again. Henry is dutiful. If she says to him that she is ready to do what he thinks proper he will not be concerned that it would be from fear, not conviction, and would at once organize everything, deeply relieved, justified in his belief in his rightness, absolved of the guilts that have gnawed him in the nights. It would give him a pastel sort of happiness in exchange for which he would persuade himself that the pale image he saw of Greece had been a mirage, not an attainable possibility. Because he, unlike Hannah, is still fighting. He hasn't acknowledged, as she has, that the war is over and nothing can be the way it was.

Meanwhile, Henry has departed, reluctant to go, desperate to get away, back to his empty castle.

"Well then," he'd said. "It seems quite adequate. Clean and comfortable. Have a good rest and I'll come and pick you up in a few days. The change will probably do you good. Then we'll see the doctor? Hmm?"

Hannah had not thought it worthwhile to go through it all again. Explanations lose their force when repeated ad nauseam. The precision of "ad nauseam" has become real to Hannah in the last days. She feels a physical sickness at the thought of another futile repetition of their positions. They don't listen to each other anymore. There's no point in telling Henry again that she's not going to be picked up in a few days, or at all, so she simply says, "Thank you for bringing me, Henry. Tell the boys they can come and see me if they like."

The moment of parting affects them both, in spite of themselves. Henry hovers, uncertain whether to touch her or not. She wishes he would go because she is tempted, in this unknown house, to say, "All right, Henry. Let's go home," and she mustn't do that, so she says instead, "Have a good journey. Phone me in a couple of days, right?"

"Right," he says finally and then goes quickly, without fuss.

So there she is, waiting, animation suspended. After a long while, she begins to feel ridiculous. She goes on sitting there, but the feeling of absurdity gets stronger, until she begins to giggle. Why on earth, she wonders, as the giggles turn to snorts of laughter, has she put on her best coat, her new shoes, and, heaven preserve us, a hat? And carrying a handbag.

"It's you again, Mother," she addresses the shade of Mrs. Owen. "And yes, I have got clean underwear on in case I have an accident and have to go to the hospital."

Such formality for a journey. She imagines herself lying in her coffin and the undertaker's men, about to nail down the lid, leaping back in alarm as she suddenly puts up a hand to stop them, squealing, "Hang on a minute. I've forgotten my handbag."

She stands and looks around the living room. It's very Edith. Very magazine-conscious, with studiedly simple furnishings. It's comfortable though, as Henry observed, and the central heating, discreetly installed as a functional encouragement to the aesthetic logs in the fireplace, has warmed it up nicely. She goes from room to room again, having already been around once with Henry, but that doesn't count. A place where you're going to be alone can't properly be examined with someone else. The kitchen is small, practical, and well equipped. Edith has confined the country charm to the living room, where it doesn't cause her unnecessary inconvenience. Hannah supposes she approves of that, though it might have been more seriously living "alone" had she had to draw water from a well and carry it in buckets.

The bedroom is pretty. Its little window looks out to the back of the cottage, across hedgerows and fields that are very plump and soft, like an eiderdown. It has rained during the day and now as the afternoon subsides into evening, the coming green of the spring is reflected in the huge sky.

"How peaceful," thinks Hannah conventionally, then shivers primevally at the hugeness of the sky and the smallness of herself and the clammy loneliness that is already lying in ambush on the edges of her mind. Frighteningly, somewhere deep and inaudible, she feels her own voice, very small, saying, "Mummy?"

She changes her clothes quickly and hurries down the stairs to the kitchen, where she turns on the lights, switches on the radio, and plugs in the kettle, establishing an evening atmosphere so that the fading light and the growing dark can't creep up and catch her unawares.

After she's eaten a sandwich she didn't want and unpacked the things she's brought, it takes no time to clear up and then she doesn't know what to do. It was a mistake to arrive late on a Sunday afternoon. She should have thought of that and insisted on getting here early in the day so that she could have walked around a bit before dark, and then, locked in for the night, she would have had some sense of her setting.

In the car Hannah had looked blankly ahead, seeing no more than the flat gray wall that is the inside of her head, relieved only by a rare recognition of trees and fields. She had vaguely observed that the landscape opened out into wide vistas with a tremendous sky, then their arrival had taken her by surprise. The little bit of road immediately outside the cottage was all she had registered and now she has no knowledge of how it relates to this or that, to the pub or the post office. The cottage is in a village, not as she had envisaged it, remotely tucked away among trees and thorns like a witch's cottage in a fairy tale, and now that she's here, the twinge of disappointment at that is changed to relief. After all, she's alone. She doesn't need to labor the point by becoming a hermit buried in inaccessible depths plumbed only by the Ordnance Survey and woodcutters' lost children.

"Perhaps I should have an early night," she says aloud and glances around apologetically because her voice sounded loud. The evening has been going for a long time. It's probably a good idea to have an early night.

When she was small, she remembers, Sunday evenings belonged to a different time scale from the rest of the week. So slow, a huge pendulum carrying them with heavy momentum inexorably but immeasurably slowly toward the poor reward of bedtime and Monday. How did she fill the evening then, while her mother listened to despairing hymns on the radio and her father looked into the fire? Reading, daydreaming, sighing, wishing, waiting. Waiting. She's back to that. Her life has slipped away in waiting, and the end of every wait has been disappointment and the start of the next wait. Oh God, what's the answer? Perhaps there isn't one. Perhaps God is a practical joker, stringing us along with promises of Heaven, be good now and wait and see what goodies will come unto you in the hereafter forever and ever, and the punch line is that there is no Heaven. And when Saint Peter, snickering into his beard, opens the pearly gates, you step through into . . . nothing, and he and God fall about laughing. Wicked old men with their cruel jokes. Not funny. Or perhaps there isn't a God at all. All a great con to keep us toeing the line. What line? Whose con? Oh God, I'm going mad, thinks Hannah.

The ringing of the telephone startles her clean out of her chair. She jumps up, quite disoriented, and has to follow the sound of the bell to find the phone. It's fixed on the wall behind the kitchen door.

"Hullo?" Hannah is nervous.

"Hannah? It's David."

"Oh."

"Settled in all right?"

"Oh yes. Yes. Quite settled, thank you."

"Good. Look, I'm sorry I missed you this morning. Why didn't you wait? I'd only popped out to the newsagent's."

"Yes, Christine said. I'm sorry I couldn't wait. I only looked in to say good-bye . . . I was in an awful rush."

It's not true. Hannah didn't want to see Christine or David, but felt constrained by good manners to say good-bye, with a ready-made excuse for not staying. She has begun to find Christine's calm leaden and daunting, and David's soft remorselessness makes her edgy, and besides, the last fortnight has drained her too much for social effort.

"Well, never mind. Look, I'm coming down the day after tomorrow, early. We'll get something organized about research."

"Oh . . . I don't know . . ." Hannah doesn't want that. She's beginning so much to want company that she doesn't want to risk any in case she gives in. Incredibly, only Edith would be welcome. Certainly not David.

"Nonsense. You've got plenty of time, haven't you? Edith told me you're having a change of scene while caretaking for her and showing possible buyers around. That can't occupy you too much?"

Well done, Edith. A nice, open-ended explanation, enforceable at odd hours and times and at short notice.

"But I've never done any sort of research. I'd be no use to you."

"Don't be silly. I'll persuade you. You'll have lunch, surely?"

"Well . . ."

"OK. See you Tuesday morning, about eleven. 'Bye."

And he's gone. Just like that. Hannah stares down the mouthpiece of the phone as if she expected to see him lurking there.

Oh well, she thinks, it will pass the time. If he's as pushy as usual, it'll be such a relief when he goes that I'll be glad of being left to myself!

But now, it's still only eight-thirty and it's time she did something decisive about this evening, before the nibbling fear that lives with her now makes a big enough hole to admit panic.

Should she phone Henry? Or Edith maybe? No. That would be cheating. Too easy to say it's only the first evening and she's breaking herself in gently to her new way of life. It's not a good enough excuse. No, a bath, keep the radio on, find a book, paint her toenails, search Edith's cupboards even. She does all those things and finds, like water in the desert, a pile of girlie magazines, only half hidden, in Cyril's wardrobe.

She's never seen any before, except on station bookstalls, when she has hastily averted her eyes. They're big and glossy and lavish, extravagant, sensual, thrilling. They absorb her so entirely that the evening finds itself ignored and goes away. Hannah is enthralled by the pictures. Even more enthralled by the letters. She takes the magazine to bed with her and reads on avidly, astounded at the enormity of her inexperience. Her eyes open wide at the succulent photographs, and she examines them from every angle, turning them around to see how they look the other way up, studying every detail.

Poor Henry. Does he too have a secret store of these? How can he not, if Cyril does? Do all men? No wonder wives are disappointing if this is what men are led to expect. But are these women real? Are they wives?

She reviews the wives she knows best: herself, Edith, Janet . . . oh no, it's laughable. Not one of them is of the same species as these women. These women are aware that persons may be men, or may be women, and neither is more and neither is less. A woman may be a wife, but as well as, not instead of, a person.

"Here we are," they say. "This is the way we are, isn't it nice? Nice for us, nice for you. We'll do what we can to please you, and you do what you can to please us. Everybody's happy. Interdependence, that's what it's all about. Not competition. In competitions you can't have a winner without having a lot of losers. Hardly anybody's happy. Now, observe our bodies of mother-of-pearl and gold. Consider how our softness and smoothness complement your hardness and roughness. Aren't we pretty? Don't we make you feel good?"

Oh poor Henry. Assuredly neither Hannah nor garden gnomes have ever fulfilled his needs as these could. And the letters. Is this how people live? People who are alive and informed? Twitching with annoyance at the extent of her naïveté, Hannah devours the magazines until her eyes grow too heavy and she falls asleep untroubled by the quiet night, thinking carnal thoughts, stretching herself out across the bed, inviting richly fantastic visitations, instead of curled up as usual in her fetal innocence.

She dreams fleshly dreams, where jewel-colored snakes rise up to turn into pillars of smoke rearing mightily from railway engines as they vanish with a thrilling rush into dark tunnels.

Thirteen

She wakes refreshed and enjoys the recollection of her dreams, though ruefully, because although the shadow is something, the substance has eluded her, and now it's too late to do anything about it. What a pity. But still she smiles as she dresses, and the erotic images lodge lightly at the back of her mind. It's a fine morning. She walks through the village before breakfast. There's a green and a pretty church with yew trees, a bridge over a little stream, and a bakery where she buys new bread. She says good morning to strangers, and the man in the bakery talks to her as he serves her. He's never seen or heard of Henry. Whatever he makes of Hannah will be quite fresh, his conclusions uncluttered by Henry or Mrs. Owen, he'll never call her "Mother" because he can't be bothered to look up her name on a card, he'll never dismiss her as somebody's daughter, or somebody's wife, or somebody's mother. To him she's somebody herself. That's nice, thinks Hannah.

She goes back to the cottage for breakfast, happier than for a long while, satisfied that the cottage is safely fastened to the ground, anchored in time and space. The village exists and has shops and a post office and a pub and real people occupy it and she's one of them. She's pleased with herself. Smug almost. It rather puzzles her that she should feel renewed by vicarious thrills, objectively seeing it as disgraceful that she should benefit from sexual fantasies triggered by commercial photography. She reflects on this but then decides there's no reason to spoil her own fun by being puritan or analytical. Prurience before prudence, she says to herself solemnly and laughs as she resumes her study of the magazines over breakfast. She has a holiday feeling, something she's lost since her sons grew away. She remembers feeling like this when they were small and she'd planned a treat for them. A whole day of indulgence for the three of them. Living out some fairy tale. Dangerous nonsense, God knew what it might lead to, Henry said without specifying, so that Hannah was left wondering what he meant and determined not to ask. As far as she knows, she reflects complacently, since then armed with a little more general knowledge, both her sons are quite enthusiastically heterosexual, though naturally they never talk to her about such things, and she's never talked to them about such things. Naturally. That was up to Henry. Naturally. Now there's a thought. She puts down her cup slowly and stares at it, her complacency evaporating. Why did she never talk to them about love, about men and women? About caring?

Hannah shakes her head, unwilling to admit guilt, but guilt has gained a toehold. She, with so much power, said nothing, did nothing, to make them tender toward people, to make them care imaginatively, and not to label people Man or Woman. Accepting her own subservience, though so unwillingly, in the one area where she did have power, she simply hadn't bothered to use it, hadn't even recognized she had it to use. She should have explained to them, instilled into them that people, men, women, should not wither away into wives and husbands for lack of imagination. Failed. Oh damn. Hannah throws her magazines on the floor. Instead of constructively destroying the pattern through her sons, she conformed to it blindly. Playing games was lovely, but she should have had more thought for real people and less for fairy creatures. Did Henry see that? Did he dimly perceive what she did not, that the children could have been a bridge between them, instead of a chasm? They could have shared the children. They both loved them enough. But instead they built two separate camps, Mummy and Daddy, and let the poor little things scurry back and fore between them, along a path that grew narrower and narrower.

Hannah doesn't like nasty discoveries. She jumps up and clears the table in a burst of activity. The boys are the one success of her life. She will not have it that she failed them and abused them, that she evaded responsibility in the pursuit of gratification. She will not. So why then does she hear her own voice, long ago, saying to the boys time and again, "Don't bother Daddy. He's got important things to do." Important. What did she mean by that, for goodness' sake? That he had teeth to think about, and money, and stone dwarves? She had firmly labeled such things as "important" and, as a direct consequence, sons and wives as lesser, and had reestablished the pecking order for yet another generation.

Hannah wails in fury now. She doesn't want to be guilty. She wanted to know about herself, yes, but only nice, creditable things. She wished for a selective self-knowledge, to find out the admirable things, not to have it thrust repeatedly before her like this that she is not only victim, but aggressor as well.

Now an empty day lies ahead, full of empty time. Since she has only a measured amount of time, it seems absurdly contradictory to have so much of it and no idea what to do with it. "Prepare to meet thy doom," the billboards say, but how does Hannah do that, she wonders, and keep her mind off dangerous ground? It suggests lots of activity, a busy, busy bustle, a countdown. Hurry up, doom's coming, it's on its way, must finish preparing or it'll be here before I get the potatoes on.

She remembers that David's coming tomorrow and is glad. How nice to have an event, any event, to make a dent in time.

Did he mean he'd take her out to lunch, or was he expecting her to give him lunch? Should she have invited him? He ought to have said. He was the one who said he wanted people to say what they meant. Why do people so often not say what they mean, so often say nothing at all, when so many lacerated feelings and lost hopes could be saved by frankness? Well, he can take her out to lunch or they can both go hungry. Doom must please itself. It's a bleak prospect ahead. Nothing but spasms of David, long walks, and self-communing to fill the hours. She wishes she hadn't come. Henry is right. This is a silly business. She should just have stayed at home and carried on as usual, coffee-mornings, dinner parties, shopping. It would have passed the time, wouldn't it? There simply isn't enough of her to hold her interest by itself. But Edith said it was right to come. Edith ought to know about how to seek salvation. No, if Edith knew, she'd have found her own. Poor Edith. Poor Cyril. Doesn't anyone do it right? Is there a right way, or is that the secret of the universe? That we are all shadows grasping at other shadows, so it's hopeless from the start to try to find anything concrete to hold to.

She is about to give herself to tears and cry luxuriantly when the telephone rings.

"Hullo. Good morning," says David. "I'm nearly there."

"What? Where?"

"With you. I'm on my way."

Doom, thinks Hannah at once.

"But it isn't tomorrow." She wonders passingly whether she's overlooked a day.

"No, it's today. Tomorrow never comes. I changed my mind. That all right?"

"I was going for a walk," she complains, aggrieved.

"Good. I'll come with you. I'll be there in a quarter of an hour."

"But David."

"Fifteen minutes." And he was gone.

Perversely, Hannah feels she has been cheated out of a solitary walk, and that a walk was the very reason she has come here. What an irritating man, always picking at people's doings, carrying people along where they didn't want to go, overwhelming them with gentle persistence.

"I don't know." She heaves an exaggerated sigh. "What a

nuisance." But still she hurries upstairs to add the touches of this and the shades of that to her face that she hadn't bothered with earlier. Coming back into the living room, she hears a car coming along the road and at the same moment notices the scattered magazines on the table and the floor.

"Oh my goodness." She hastily gets down on all fours and starts to collect them, but they're big and slippery and will not be quickly collected by fumbling hands, they skate away to spread themselves more widely over the floor. There she is, on her hands and knees, scrabbling after them, when there's a knock at the door and it opens and David walks in.

She turns and looks up at him over her shoulder, furious and embarrassed.

"Hullo," he says.

How dare he? How dare he arrive in the first place and then not wait for his knock to be answered. How dare he catch her in such an annoying situation. How dare he catch her at all, let alone bottom-up, her hands full of pictures of naked women and pages where the words burn through onto her covering palms. She seethes with temper.

"Hullo," she says calmly, with a noncommittal smile.

"I'll help you," he replies blandly, kneeling down beside her and starting to pick up magazines.

I won't explain, Hannah informs herself. I will not comment. It's none of his business.

"I found them," she hears herself explaining feebly and wants to hit herself.

"They're fun," David remarks. "Here, look at this one."

He holds up a picture of a red-haired girl, red hair pouring over her shoulders and an almost three-dimensional triangle of red hair thrusting itself at Hannah.

"When I was a stripling, you only found photographs of naked ladies in 'health' magazines and all the pubic hair had to be shaved off. It took years of research to discover how much diversity there is in pubic hair. This lot's quite a collector's choice."

Hannah blushes and wants to kick him because a very simi-

111

lar thought had come to her last night. Pubic hair, if she'd ever given it a thought, was simply pubic hair and certainly not a subject for research. What a nasty man.

Yet she moves involuntarily inside her skirt and loathes herself.

"I found them," she repeats in a truculent mutter.

David gathers up the magazines into a stack, which Hannah needlessly pats and aligns.

"Let's go for this walk, then," David says as if, thinks Hannah, it's perfectly usual for him to be crawling about the floor looking at naughty pictures with a middle-aged woman he hardly knows. Perhaps it is. Oh dear. She looks at the magazine on top of the pile. The girl on the cover is beautiful. Smooth. An unlined face, golden body, hair shining like the coat of a healthy animal.

"She's lovely," Hannah says.

"She might grow to be," David decides, crawling over and putting a hand lightly on Hannah's shoulder as he looks at the picture. "She's too smooth yet. Like an egg. Nothing's happened behind her face."

"How odd. I thought that would appeal to a man . . . youth, firmness. Like sound fruit."

"Mmm. Sound fruit's fine. I'm a wine-and-cheese man myself. Time adds flavor and fullness. Can't rush it."

Hannah gets to her feet, wondering whether she reminds him of a moldy blue Stilton. He stands too. Hannah's thinking she hasn't the least idea what Henry thinks about women—whether he's a leg man or the other sort, whether he'd choose apples or claret. Silently she puts on her coat while David pokes about the room, looking at this and that.

"Let's go," she says shortly, distressed once more that she and Henry have wasted one another's time, wanting to hurt David because he has inadvertently picked at her sore, desolated at the uselessness of trying to do anything about anything.

They follow the road down to the center of the village, Hannah plodding along silently beside David, looking at the ground. He wears suede shoes. Lovely, soft russet suede. Her mother would never have trusted him. A completely reliable indicator of character, suede shoes. Or two-tone correspondent shoes. No trustworthy man would be seen dead in them. Hannah peeps from the corner of her eye at the beautiful, expensive clothes. Nothing extreme, nothing haphazard, everything fine and chosen. He is, she admits, a good-looking man, though not her type.

Not her type? What is she thinking of? She hasn't got a type. Isn't that one of the things that infuriates her? You have to have tried out a few and come to a conclusion before you can claim to have a type. Her fantastic companions at the dream dinners-for-two have always been faceless, voiceless, just a shadow and a presence beyond the candle flame. What she really means is that she simply hasn't considered David as a candidate for fantasy. The men she sees regularly, Henry, Cyril, George, the husbands, have never presented themselves as worth spending a dream on. She's never given it a thought. Husbands are just not dream material. Even before they married, Henry hadn't fitted the Lover mold. Not Hannah's, anyway.

David couldn't be more unlike Henry in appearance. Where Henry is heavy and dark, bulky and blurred, high-colored, David is all clear, clean lines. His face is narrow, his nose is narrow, his eyes are light, and his hair is like the coat of a well-fed fox, not oily but with a smooth gloss.

"What are you thinking about?" he asks suddenly.

Hannah blushes and hastily covers up her thoughts.

"Nothing," she answers with a false smile.

"The first time we met," David continues, "at Edith's dinner, you were detached, with a kind of lofty, observing calm, very much your own person in spite of what you said. Now you're defensive. Not so much detached as concealed."

He doesn't ask why. It's an observation, not a query. Hannah thinks about it. He's right of course. Two weeks ago, a little more, she was exalted, filled with confidence and importance, calling the tune. Only, after a few exploratory hops, no one, that is Henry, has danced. And exaltation, unfed and unwatered, has withered. But that won't do. Here she is, she's taken a step, made a decision, and acted on it, although she concedes that without Edith's push she probably wouldn't have. Clearly, she must reestablish exaltation. Here she is, with a man, a very attractive man, on a spring morning early in the rest of her life. She looks up at him and smiles.

"I was thinking how nice to walk in an unfamiliar place with an attractive man."

He grins.

"Better. Let's go and have a drink and see where we go from here."

They find the village pub, quiet on a Monday morning with only the old men of the village communing with their beer and carrying on the desultory conversation in shorthand they have been having for years.

David produces a notebook and starts telling Hannah the sort of thing he wants her to do. Making the acquaintance of people in the village, asking them to recall family anecdotes, letting them talk.

"I can't go far afield, you know. I haven't got a car."

"Never mind. I'll be down often to visit and to have a look at houses. I've got a list. There's a deadline to meet, so I'll be concentrating on it."

"How's Christine?"

"What? Oh. Oh, she's fine. Now, can you clear this first bit for me by, say, the end of the week?" He holds out a list of possible openings and questions.

"I suppose so. Does Christine help you sometimes? Why didn't she come with you?"

He puts his notebook away, goes to the bar, buys them another drink, comes back, sits down, lights a cigarette for each of them, blows a plume of smoke at the ceiling. Hannah feels a quiver of anticipation. He's trying to make her back-pedal, fluster her, put her out of countenance, change the subject. Well, she won't. She won't say another word until after he does. She sips her drink, smokes her cigarette, wondering why she feels her party spirit reviving.

The silence goes on. He regards her through smoke, she returns his gaze. Then at last, "Why do you want to know?"

114

Clever. Hannah's won her tiny victory . . . he spoke first . . . but its flavor is diluted because he hasn't answered her question. She doesn't, she realizes blithely, care a jot why Christine hasn't come. She's glad she hasn't come, but she wants answers when she asks questions.

All right, if this is a game, she'll play.

"I don't want to know, beyond a touch of inquisitiveness. I do want to know why you don't want to tell."

He smiles and nods, but doesn't answer that either.

They are benign together, the game has been established and may be resumed at any time. In the meanwhile there's plenty to talk about. David has been everywhere, met people, tells it all amusingly. Hannah laughs often, and her listening face is alive. David is intrigued by her response. Her reactions are slanted away from the line he had anticipated. She is not aggressively feminine or competitive, but there is a veiled force of aggression in her that he feels strongly.

The day goes by, and with it Hannah's slipping hold on exaltation regains strength. She doesn't think of the empty evening and all the other empty evenings. She's on the mountain, skipping among the wild flowers, the sun is warm on the rocks and the Wolf is only a black spot at the back of her mind, to be faced when he comes. But not yet. Later. Poor Hannah, she won't let herself remember that the Wolf is not make-believe, a bogey to scare little children into being good.

Evening gets closer, but the air on the mountain stays sweet, the scent of the flowers isn't diminished, their colors fade but still glow pale against the dusk. Hannah is having a lovely time, he smiles at her with approval and weighs her opinions in the same balance as his own. He measures her words with the same yardstick as his own. She fills out, grows plump with confidence, like a currant soaked in wine.

When it's nearly dark, they go back to the cottage, and David orders, "Change your clothes. Put something pretty on and we'll go and have dinner somewhere."

"But David, that'll make it dreadfully late for you to drive back. I was thinking a quick sandwich . . ."

He puts his hands on her shoulders.

"But I'm not going back."

She is about to say something silly, like "Where will you stay?" when his meaning penetrates, so she says nothing but looks back at him, seeing that he has one long hair growing in the middle of one eyebrow, that there is a tempting blackhead near the corner of one eye, that his lips are thin and well defined, that his skin is smooth and has a golden cast. And thus Hannah, playing her game of cosmic find-the-lady, has turned over the right card. A tremor of conscience, a nudge from her mother's shade, a warmth like warm honey softening her skin, nice, kind God saying, "Come along, dear, it's your turn now."

"All right," she says.

Fourteen

Hannah wakes in the night. The window is barely lighter than the opaque blackness outside . . . there are no street lights . . . and for an instant she wonders where she is. How marvelous to wake like this, knowing you're happy. Big and heavy with contentment, relaxed into bonelessness. David lies beside her, asleep. Not at all like a crusader, David. He lies on his chest, his head turned on the pillow, one arm stretched out across Hannah's shoulder. Funny, that. Awake, he's so neat, so contained, clear-cut. Asleep, he's floppy, all loose ends. The very reverse of Henry, who sleeps so tidily, rigidly at attention, and battles when awake to hold himself together.

She ought to think she's dreaming, but she knows she isn't. It's true, and her conscience doesn't trouble her in the least. She did feel it should, even worried a little that she wasn't worried when she ought to be, but overriding everything is the insistent repetition, "It's my turn."

Why not, after all? An adventure, no strings, no complications, and who's to know, anyway? David's almost a stranger, but he's clean, and good-looking, amusing though irritating. And besides, she can't seem to resist him. Certainly no one's going to be hurt, so where's the harm? And she has to take her turn as and when she can before she misses it altogether.

117

An adventure in living for her isn't going to hurt Christine or do any more damage to Henry. Hannah reflects on the past evening, lying beside this man whom she supposes is her lover. Alien word.

David says, "I'm not going back."

She replies, "All right."

So easy, in the event, to lift both feet off the bottom and swim.

Then he says, "Good. Now let's find somewhere to eat."

"I've nothing to wear. I didn't bring anything for dining out. I wasn't expecting to be dining out."

"You should always allow for unexpected events. Still, never mind."

"No, no. Wait a minute," says Hannah. "I'll wear my dressing gown."

She hurries upstairs and while David drinks his own whisky, she paints her face quite vividly and brushes her hair up and back until her head pleases her very much. She turns this way and that before the mirror, trying out a few pouts and siren glances. The bones in her face stand out proudly and her eyes shine with an anticipatory, almost predatory glitter. But there's the problem of underwear. And the unlovely manifestations of her disease. What is she to do? There's no question of telling David about the cancer. It's not catching, and anyway there are other diseases that are and if he were worried about catching things, he wouldn't do this kind of thing. For she doesn't deceive herself there: he's a practiced man. No, as for that, she'll just have to hope for the best. But underwear. That really is serious. She feels very cross indeed that she has such sensible, functional, chain-store underwear. Quite pretty. A far cry from interlock knickers, but satin, satin, that's what she should have. Oh the lovely satin knickers. If only she could conjure them from the past now, slippery, asking to be touched, sliding against her skin. Till now, only Mrs. Owen has been able to drum up any serious interest in Hannah's knickers, and then for reasons of durability and protection, not excitement. Now, out of nowhere, knickers are paramount.

She casts her mind ahead to later, much later, this evening, and realizes she hasn't the least idea of how it's done. She's never even read a textbook: *Teach Yourself Adultery. Lesson One: Undressing.*

Oh dear, oh dear. She can't bear the idea of a brisk, schoolgirl business. Shouldn't she be thinking in terms of a seductive strip? But you need music and black stockings for that, don't you? Oh dear. Her girdle leaves a mark around her waist, and how are you supposed to take off a girdle and tights seductively? In the bathroom, of course. Of course. What a relief. It's obvious. And then you come gliding into the twilit bedroom in a beautiful nightgown.

Not, oh for heaven's sake, not in a sensible, long-sleeved, fleecy effort.

Oh, oh. I should have had time to prepare for this, thinks Hannah, distraught, and before she can change her mind, she flings on the red robe over nothing but her bra, which by lucky chance is rather nice because she has a tiny bust and buys in the teen-age department.

She puts on her good, plain, go-with-anything court shoes, and without daring to meet her own eyes in the mirror leaves the room.

David looks up as she comes in, then he rises and comes toward her.

"Beautiful," he says.

Hannah is astounded. Firstly, she knows she's not, at least she doesn't think so, well, no one's ever mentioned it, and her mother would say it wasn't quite nice. Secondly, in her experience, it isn't the sort of thing men actually say, outside of films. There she goes again, "in her experience." What experience? The most generous compliment from Henry is "You look nice" or, if he's really carried away, "very nice." Is that experience?

Well, she's going to enjoy this. If he says extravagant things, he doesn't have to mean them and she doesn't have to believe them, but it gives her a ruby warmth to hear them.

"Good idea, the dressing gown," says David. "I'll have a shave and change my shirt, then we'll be off."

He goes upstairs, quite at ease. He's got a small suitcase. He's fully equipped. He knew he was staying the night.

Somewhere.

But where?

Naturally, in his work, overnight stops are routine. There's always a suitcase ready in his car. Hannah drops into a chair, feeling as if she's made of ice, and the ice is breaking up into bits that will melt into a grimy puddle on the floor.

He never said he'd be staying with her. It was she who leaped to that conclusion, projecting into reality wishes she didn't even know she had. Oh my Lord, she thinks. Thank God I didn't actually say anything. I would die of shame. But what horror and misery fills her now, sitting there with her painted face and no knickers, how staggeringly, unspeakably stupid. She has to hold her head very high so that the tears that fill her eyes don't run and ruin her careful makeup. The insanity of thinking he'd want to sleep with her, the stupendous arrogance of assuming that a smooth, experienced man, years younger than she, could have entertained such a thought. How he'd laugh if he knew what she'd been thinking. Perhaps this minute, in the bathroom, he's holding a towel against his mouth to stifle the guffaws, heaving with mirth at the poor, naïve, pathetic old hag. . . .

She gets up and pours herself a very large whisky. She hates whisky, but it's all there is and she needs something to wash away the humiliation that soils her. Until he comes down, she sits quite still, drinking the whisky deliberately, without a shudder, and clinging by her fingernails to the chance that he doesn't realize what she'd thought and that consequently they may have an amiable evening. The day was pleasant. More than that. It was the easy companionship of the day that caused her to forget herself and think she was involved in a real relationship with another person. Something beyond an exchange of platitudes. It may be a real enough relationship but she's ashamed to think that having been given an inch she knew no better than to grab for a mile. She must content herself with her inch. It's after all an important inch more than she had before. The whisky is warming her and softening the cutting edges of ice in her stomach. She feels a little better: if she could be assured that he hasn't guessed her overreaching, the ease of the day can maybe be retrieved and extended.

She'd like to go upstairs and slip on knickers and tights. It would be much more comfortable and she wouldn't have the constant reminder of her folly, but now the bathroom door is opening and David's coming back. She gulps the last of her whisky and prepares to face him.

But she can't look directly at him. It's too shaming. So she stands with her back to the door, looking out through the window. It's quite dark now and the cottages in the street are cozily curled up for the night, like puppies.

"It's quite dark," she says, knowing he's in the room. He moves so quietly, not thump, thump, thump, like Henry, but light on his feet like an elegant fox. He reminds her of a fox. She smells that he's close behind her. Aftershave. Oddly, he uses the same one as Henry, but it's different on him, not a smelling-salts attack, but a pervasive delicacy that makes her want to breathe him in.

Sadly, defeatedly, she admits to herself that she wanted to lie with him, still wants to. Juvenile it may be, but she has no sensual history. There's a hole in her experience that only a sensual adventure can fill. David by chance strayed into her path and without knowing it, she thought he could, would, lend himself to her purpose. She has in large measure misled herself about her motives for wishing to live alone. Alone means apart from Henry. Apart from Henry means liberty to embark on new courses if they present themselves. She has tried to be honest, but you can't tell the whole truth without being in possession of all the facts, and some of the facts about herself are buried deeper than she knew and are surfacing piecemeal, like wreckage. She wanted romance, an excitement.

His hands touch her shoulders.

"You've gone away," he says. "Why?"

There's no answer she can make to that. She can't say, "I thought you wanted me, but you don't, and I do want you but didn't know it till I'd realized my mistake, so it's all a silly nothing and I should have known better."

"Hannah," he says very quietly and his hands tighten on her shoulders and pull her gently to lean on him. She doesn't resist. She's too sad. If he offers a little comfort, she'll take it and be grateful.

"Hannah, come back."

He turns her to face him. She stares at him for a second, solemn, then unable to bear the questioning of his eyes, not blue, not green, she closes hers and says nothing. He puts his arms around her and presses her head to his chest so that the smell of him fills her nostrils and makes her wearily furious.

She wants him. She wants him very much indeed. A new stimulus she was more comfortable without. But he needn't think he's irresistible, even though he sees her need. She can do without, thank you very much. No need for charity.

"You don't have to be kind," she says, pulling away, intending to sound cold and controlled, and failing.

He doesn't answer immediately, then, "I'm not a kind man, Hannah. I don't have to be kind to anybody. We've had a good day. Let's not spoil it."

She sighs.

"No. All right."

She looks at him then, and he's smiling at her. His mouth is beautiful, and a streak of white light shoots inside Hannah from her groin to her throat.

Oh my God, she thinks, feeling her mouth slack and her body heavy and knowing that she can't control the urge to touch him, though she must. But his arms are around her again and he's pressing her close to him. She lifts her head and enters into his kiss. She concentrates on what's happening because she'll need to remember it later and live on it. His tongue is inside her mouth. She's always thought of that as horrid. But now it's not. It's marvelous. Her tongue ventures out to meet his. Lovely, lovely. Her arms go around his neck and she holds tightly, his hands warmly, securely caressing her body, shaping it to fit his. Every inch of her has a corresponding inch of him. It's marvelous. Unbelievable. She wants more, lots more. The kiss ends and Hannah nearly falls, but David supports her and sets her tidily on her feet.

"Oh dear," she says, then laughs, out of breath. "Sorry."

"Sorry? You are an idiot." Suddenly he's brisk. "Come on, I'm starving. That was an aperitif. Whetted my appetite."

What does he mean? Hannah is slowly coming back to herself. Was it just an ordinary kiss to him? Does it mean anything at all? Or was it just a sweet for an importunate child?

"David," she hears her voice saying and is astounded at her temerity. "Please don't play games with me. I don't know how to play. I've never learned."

He takes both her hands in his and though he's smiling, he's not joking.

"I'm not playing with you. I thought you'd understood that. You're a lovely woman and I've been drawn to you since we met at Edith's. I'm physically aware of you all the time. OK? Can we take it from there?"

Hannah tries to see into his head to see if he's telling the truth. The not blue, not green eyes don't evade her. He withstands her scrutiny without fuss. She thinks she can see truth. He says he isn't kind, but she doesn't believe that, and she does want him so badly, and more of his kisses, enough to make up for all the years. She wants him to say more, to make promises that she can snuggle into, but he's saying nothing, merely waiting for her answer. She judges him and finds in his favor.

"Yes, please," she says.

"Come on then."

He brings her a coat and puts it around her shoulders, gravely tweaking it into place like a clumsy nanny. He tucks her tenderly into the car and they drive down narrow lanes, tunnels between hedgerows, the heater humming softly, the lights opening up a way for them. Hannah feels unreal and, at the same time, more real than ever in her life before, quite sure that she is, in fact, Hannah Jackson sitting here, but being coolly observed too by the same, said Hannah Jackson. She puts it down to the whisky. She had better put everything down to the whisky because, now that the moment is over, she realizes that he didn't after all tell her what, as Mrs. Owen would put it, His Intentions are.

They drive in silence, passing through tiny deserted villages, each with an inordinately large church, square tower dominating hunched cottages.

"To the glory of God, or to appease Him," David muses.

"Do you believe in God?" Hannah asks. It seems unlikely that he should.

"What do you mean by God?"

Hannah is suddenly provoked beyond civility.

"Why do you never answer a question? What is so risky about giving a civil answer? Do you believe in God? Why isn't Christine with you? Do you want to go to bed with me?"

Her hand flies to her mouth to stop the outpouring. Now he'll very likely stop the car, make her get out and walk, and she's lost him before finding out if she had him, even on the most tenuous, short-term basis. The car goes on, the headlights continue to bore a tunnel through the darkness. A rabbit's eyes flash, mad-green, and are gone. Hannah yearns for knickers, hot cocoa, feet in slippers before the television.

They arrive at a town, old streets, old houses leaning close overhead, and then at a square, empty except for a few young people waiting for adulthood and escape and filling in the time with dispirited horseplay around the closed shops. In the square is a hotel, an old coaching inn, benevolent and welcoming in the evening, a promise of comfort for travelers, ease and good food and quiet voices and, later, soft, warm beds.

"This place is supposed to be good," David says, drawing up outside and switching off the engine.

The quiet whistles into the car, insisting on being noticed, and Hannah doesn't know what to do about it. Apologize? Run away? Knickerless in the night, miles from home, how can she?

"Come on. Let's have a look at it," David says, exactly as if they had been chatting about this and that.

He comes around and opens her door and she endures being helped out, his hand firm and warm on hers. She wants to be with him, she is so grateful he hasn't tossed her away that she could cover his hands with kisses. But her grievance remains lodged firmly in her throat. She must just discipline herself, that's all, and say nothing more. . . . Goodness me, she's had enough practice. She waits obediently while he locks the car, puts an arm around her shoulders, affectionate. Loverlike? They walk to the door of the hotel.

Oh thank you, thank you, she sings inside, for putting your arm around me, touching me, not brushing me off, and to her despair, she complains aloud, "You have to tell me. I have to know."

He walks on as if he hasn't heard and sniffs appreciatively as he opens the door and they go in and delicious dinner smells and sounds waft toward them as a waiter comes into the hall from the dining room.

"Hungry?" he asks, as if he hasn't heard her.

She nods helplessly. She's not hungry now. She was. Before that she wasn't. She's been hungry and not hungry a great many times already this evening. He's bad for her digestion, if nothing else.

He ushers her into the bar and asks for the menu while they drink. Hannah is acutely miserable, staring into her gin, sitting in the corner of the long settee while he sits far away in the other corner, reading the menu. Like a distanced married couple. The first drink disappears and she doesn't even feel it, or notice a second one arrive.

Henry would be fussily assessing the relative worth and risks of the dishes by now. Pâté Maison . . . too risky . . . God knows what's in it. Better start with avocado, recognizable, identifiable, or maybe smoked salmon . . . Good God, not at that price . . . and steak to follow. Plain grilled. Sauces, no thank you . . . a good piece of meat shouldn't need messing with, and sauces are an unknown quantity, eh? Could be anything.

Unexpectedly, Hannah yearns for Henry. His conversation, his predictability, so maddening, suddenly have great charm. One knew where one was. What a comfort. One could cherish one's discontent so much more thoroughly when one could concentrate one's mind on it, without having to spare a worry for incidentals.

David leaves the corner of the settee and moves up to sit beside her, but she's drawn into herself now, indulging herself in regrets, thinking of Henry as if he were a friend from long ago.

"What would you like to start with?"

"What? Oh, anything. Whatever you're having."

"Snails."

"I don't like snails."

"Then don't have them. Look at the menu. What do you want?"

"I want to go home."

"Why?"

"Because I'm too sad to be out."

"What would you do at home?"

"Cry."

He makes her look at him, and tears of self-pity and grievous disappointment flood her eyes.

"Don't cry, Hannah." David's voice is gentle. Tender. Why not? It's not costing him anything.

"I'm not crying. Don't be so patronizing. I don't need charity. I don't need you. I don't need anyone."

The tears are on the point of overflowing and Hannah is torn between fury at so exposing herself to David and a fierce need to abandon all control, sob unrestrainedly, weep loudly, and make a totally stirred-up palette of her face to match the mess of her feelings.

David leans toward her, blocking out the rest of the room, discreetly shielding her. She helps herself to his handkerchief and blows her nose, sniffs, blinks, then folds her hands neatly in her lap and stares at them. How close he is. How warm. How hard to resist putting her head on his chest and drawing comfort and excitement from him. How futile to think of it.

"Better now?"

She nods, sniffs again, and wishes she could recapture anger because there's a spark of perverse pleasure in anger and there's no pleasure at all in this desolation.

"Hannah, Hannah. How you fight yourself. Call a truce. Let's have a good dinner, some wine, and then . . ."

Hannah holds her breath.

". . . then I'll take you home."

Impossible to eat feeling like this. Her throat will not function. Swallowing anything will be beyond her power. Mute, she raises her eyes and looks at him, fixing her attention on the long hair growing out of his eyebrow, using her will as a bludgeon to force herself into acquiescence, to control herself so that she may at least be left with his company.

It takes several seconds, but he waits, and at last she's able to say, "Avocado, and then poached salmon. Please."

He smiles then. Hannah, disciplining herself mercilessly, makes her mouth smile back.

When they stand to go to the dining room, the bar swings around, the big settees rock, and Hannah almost falls. David's arm is there, supporting her. She's horribly embarrassed. Not only throwing herself at him, but drunk besides. A disgrace to her upbringing. All that's left to her now is to get through the meal with as much dignity as she can muster and then bid him a gracious good night and good-bye and make sure their acquaintance ends there.

The dining room is dimly lit, candles on the tables, quiet couples. No clatter. No loud voices. Soothing. What perfection it could have been.

In the kind light, Hannah and David are both enhanced, the planes and hollows of their faces accentuated, their pupils dilated, imperfections faded out.

David orders, speaks to the wine steward, then, business over, leans across the table and puts his hand on it, palm upward. Hannah looks at it with interest. Not a very big hand. Clean, of course, but not shrieking antiseptically like Henry's. Slowly she puts her hand in his and his fingers close around hers and hold.

"I don't know how to behave," she says at last, her resolve to be controlled and uncommunicative evaporating.

"There isn't a set procedure. It's not a game, darling."

Darling.

"What did you say?"

"Here's your avocado coming."

What's happening? Is saying it's not a game a part of the game? And *darling*. When the boys were tiny, she used to croon to them, darling . . . darling . . . darling. It meant . . . what? That they were precious to her, an utterance of love. Does David use the word indiscriminately, as a variant to calling people by their names, a theatrical nothing? She looks from him to the avocado that's been put in front of her, then back to his face, still smiling at her.

"Darling Hannah. Eat up like a good girl."

She picks up her spoon, digs into the perfect, delicate green flesh, then puts it down again.

"David . . ."

"We're going home after dinner, and we'll go to bed, and it will be very, very good. Unless, of course, you'd rather not."

"Oh."

"You really are anxious, aren't you?" He's intrigued. Quite puzzled at her.

It's ridiculous to continue like this. Hannah can't go on floundering out of her depth any longer.

"David. I'm entirely without experience. I'm forty-two and finding out just how naïve I am. I've never . . . been with . . . any man other than Henry. I don't know how to behave or how to interpret hints, or how to draw inferences, or anything. If you've been thinking I'm something I'm not, I'm sorry, truly. But this is the way I am, and if you want to leave it at that, well, I'd have to ask you to drive me home, but that can be the end of it."

"And if I want to take it rather than leave it?" His look has become direct, unsmiling.

They regard each other gravely. At last the presence beyond the candle flame has a face. This time, it's Hannah who doesn't answer. He isn't joking or being flippant or provocative. Would he care, she wonders, if she refused him? In the core of common sense her mother left her, Hannah guesses he wouldn't. She's not the only fish in the sea. Plenty more where she came from. Christine, for a start. Edith?

Janet? Fish are two a penny, are they not? No, he wouldn't care, beyond a minimal pinprick in his pride. But she would. Oh, she would care.

Right. She's put her cards on the table. She feels much better for that. That must be one of the tricks of the game, frankness, then you don't have to remember what lies you've told, can't trip yourself up. He's been frank too, after his fashion.

Ah, there it is.

His fashion. His frankness. She's been pressing him for her kind of frankness, believing there to be only one kind. It wasn't arrogant of her. Lack of experience, lack of thought. Honesty not arrogance. She had simply overlooked the need to establish that they were both using the same language. He has frankly shown that he's interested in her body and her company. And since she frankly wants him, then that's it. Her terms, his terms, does it matter as long as understanding is reached? A brilliant smile of reprieve blossoms on her face. She's learning to play.

"I love avocado."

He nods and smiles.

Later, in the half dark of the bedroom, they stand and look at each other.

Hannah says, "I don't know what to do."

"I'll help you."

"I'll have to take my face off. I'll look old."

"No. You'll look beautiful."

All the colors come away onto tissues, and when it's done, she sees that he's right. She has a kind of beauty. Her features are the same, but her expression makes her beautiful.

She gets quickly into bed and closes her eyes when he comes and sits, un-self-consciously naked, beside her.

"You funny creature, Hannah." He laughs. "So Victorian. As if you'd never seen a naked man before."

Well, she hasn't, except for Henry, and that wasn't the same.

He remembers, and says, "Don't be shy, my love."

This is the way it's played, Hannah reminds herself. Like

the formal statements in card games. Declarations, but only in the context of the game. Remember now. This is now, while it lasts, no longer. So she laughs too, because it's funny. And it's fun. Wonderful fun as he begins to play on her body like a musician on an instrument, doing unimagined things that make the objective, observing Hannah, watching from outside, shut her eyes tightly in outraged modesty.

Henry comes and goes in Hannah's thoughts: he never did this. Or that. I'd have loathed it. Then a sense of delicacy stops her: it's an ugly, graceless thing to do, to compare. Time goes by unmeasured, fun gives way to something else to which Hannah can put no name, and then she's lost. The world could end and she would neither know nor care. There could be no better time for it, because the ideal has been achieved.

She hears herself cry out, she hears him moan, she clutches him to her ferociously. No one shall have him. She's going to keep him forever and ever.

"My love, my darling, my baby," she croons as he relaxes at last and lies exhausted with her arms closely holding him, and she thanks God that she didn't know, through all the waiting years, what she was missing, because that would have made them intolerable.

He lies still for a long time and Hannah is totally peaceful. Then, "Coffee," he says out of the blue. "Let's have coffee. No, wine."

He leaps up, refreshed, to scuffle in his suitcase and produce a bottle of wine. She watches him lovingly, reminded but not perturbed that he is younger than she is, not questioning that he should carry wine with his pajamas.

"It's not champagne, but it sparkles. We'll pretend."

They sit side by side in bed, sipping wine, and Hannah with her passion for explanation has to try to make clear to him her confusions and her wonder and her gratitude, and doesn't notice that he doesn't want to hear.

An image springs to her mind of herself and Henry, sitting side by side in bed, miles apart, drinking cocoa and reading their library books. Oh, Henry, dear Henry, she thinks. I wish you could have this too. I hope you'll find someone. You deserve this too. We all deserve it, surely, otherwise we wouldn't have been given the capacity, would we?

When David falls asleep, she tucks him up lovingly, like her babies, before she too sleeps.

Fifteen

In the morning, Hannah wakes and sees the world beginning. It's the start of time. And it isn't only the start of the rest of the rest of her life, but of a whole new existence, bright and polished, no tarnish, no dents, no scratches, shiny and brand new.

"I feel," she says to David, "virginal."

He laughs loudly. His hands move over her and she's quite conscious that a great deal of practice is involved in achieving such excellence in execution, but she doesn't mind that. She is, she considers with untested self-approval, perfectly able to rejoice in superlative performance without giving thought to the slow process of repetition that leads to it.

"All right, then. Not virginal. Like the Water Baby when the prickles fell off and he was silky smooth and reborn. All the agonies over and only lovely things to come."

He laughs again and kisses her.

"Love," he says casually and puts a pinhead of tarnish on her shiny new world.

"David?"

"Hmm?"

She knows she mustn't ask. I don't mind, she assures herself. Really I don't. It isn't the least bit important. Dangerous to ask. Alienating. Why take risks, just out of curiosity? Because her curiosity is too strong.

"Does it mean anything? I mean, last night . . . and just now . . . you said 'love,' and I wondered, well, if it meant anything . . . oh dear, no. Forget I asked. Tell me what you were like as a little boy. Were you ever a little boy?"

She puts on a childish voice and overdoes it so that she sounds embarrassingly silly. Oh damn, she says to herself and watches his face slyly to see whether his lip has curled in distaste. It hasn't. He's watching her, and his expression isn't disgusted but quite kindly and interested.

"Is it important?" he asks.

"No, no. Forget it." But she's saddened, because it is.

That's right, she chides herself bitterly. Pester him for jam when he's given you good bread and butter. Only that's oversimplifying. It's more a seeking to complete the physical excellence, because she can understand now how one aspect of contact complements the other.

Interrupting her train of thought, David says, "You want me to commit myself to you, is that it?"

She stiffens and lies very still, even her breathing slowing down.

He pulls her close, cradles her like a child.

"You make me feel protective. There's something I can't isolate about you that reminds me of a child whistling in the dark. But love? Come on, Hannah. Let's be realistic and enjoy what we have. It's a lot. I can't pretend to things I don't feel, but I promise I won't lie to you or hurt you."

Edith. A red warning winks and Hannah doesn't notice it.

She has to acknowledge that he's said a great deal. He's been generous and she's grateful. She doesn't understand why she's forcing issues, she clearly sees that she's being unreasonable, but she doesn't feel she is. Certainly he's given her something she wanted desperately, but he did it voluntarily and took pleasure in it. He gave it in large measure to please himself. She has given him all she had to give, all the subdued years, the suppressed energy, the response never before asked for in the right language.

Their mutual possession has moved her beyond under-standing. If he remains quite uncommitted and goes his way, he takes with him an essential part of herself. Struggling hard for objectivity, she concedes that her feeling is absurdly ro-mantic and that she can't expect to impose it on him. But he's no longer an adventure, there are strings, she wants to be bound by them, and she doesn't want him to go, having given her her allowance of him, leaving her incomplete to continue with her life as best she can.

Involvement. That's what she wants from him. That at the very least.

"Do you love Christine?" she asks, aware of playing with fire.

He doesn't move but she knows he has removed himself from her, put distance between them.

"Hannah," he says, a hard edge in his voice, "don't do this."

"I'm sorry, I'm sorry," she babbles, turning her face to his shoulder, kissing his neck, raising herself to cover him with kisses, to put out the fire before it burns her, frantic not to alienate him.

"Don't be cross. Please don't be cross, David."

He warms to her again.

"There, it's all right, Hannah, it's all right. Don't get so upset."

He soothes her, taking time and pains over it so that she feels he must care, otherwise he wouldn't bother. She re-sponds to every move he makes, wanting to please him, to give him the same intensity of pleasure he gives her, to make herself indispensable to him, to blot from his memory all the others who have been or who might be, so that she, Hannah, can be the focal point in his consciousness. She discovers in herself a talent for abandon and inventiveness that later, when she can think coolly, amazes her and causes her some self-satisfaction.

David at last lies quiet, replete, and Hannah watches him. Fox. Auburn and gold. Hers. He has to belong.

"My love," she croons. "My love, my treasure."

And instantly, it's true. He is the instrument of her delight, the vehicle for her new skill, therefore she loves him. Not like her babies, but yes, like her babies in that his existence and her involvement with his body are reason enough for love.

"I must go soon," he mumbles, nearly asleep.

Her heart sinks, but she's almost sure now that he'll come back, not just to complete his research. She can make herself settle for that, she thinks. Love him without chains, forbid herself to think of him with Christine. Christine. What is the truth of Christine? No. She bars the question. None of her business. Another world. Here, with Hannah, he exists, and that must be enough.

This is a dreadfully hard game to master. The apparent simplicity of the moves masks the subtlety of the concept. But she'll learn. It's worth it. She'll do it right this time.

After he's gone she's both sad and happy. Contented because he's said he'll be back in three days, sad because he's not with her, glad of time to prepare for his return, reluctant to wash away the bloom of their contact.

She floats through the day, murmuring his name over and over till it loses touch with the actual man and becomes a mantra.

She savors again in retrospect the taste of every good moment, adjusts the bad moments into amusing steps along the path to the rainbow's end, and turns their chance coming together into inevitability. Whether or not she actually knows or likes him has become immaterial: she loves what he alone has made her feel and equates that, girllike, with loving him. Knowing how much there is still to know, she still falls into the trap. She leaps into it eagerly. She wants to be in love, romantic, hearts-and-flowers, poems-and-love-songs love. None of it has anything to do with marriage, or paying bills, or making sure there is soap in the bathroom. The world she is willfully trying to bring into being is peopled with elegant creatures who never have head colds or need their teeth filled. It's a world of celebration.

The coming of evening takes her by surprise; the afternoon

has slipped her notice, absorbed as she has been in exploring new dimensions and in fashioning her pipe dream of being in love.

She's sitting, entranced, gazing at the logs in the fireplace, when David phones.

"Hullo. What are you wearing?"

"My dressing gown. Why?"

"I want to imagine you."

"Oh. That's nice. I've been imagining you."

"Hannah?" He sounds diffident.

"Yes, David?"

"I find I'm missing you."

Warmth fills her, flowing rosily right through her, but she manages to restrain gladness and keep her excitement within bounds.

"I'm missing you too. I'm so glad you're coming again on Friday."

She succeeds in biting back the question. She must wait for him to say whether or not he'll be staying. No pressure. Still, she sends a wave of will down the telephone.

"Hannah?"

"Yes?"

"Take care, darling." It's almost her undoing. She hugs herself, overflowing with pride, wanting to laugh out loud with happiness. He sounds so . . . loving. That is the right word. She's sure. May she then permit herself an endearment?

"Are you still there?" he asks.

"Yes, I'm still here. Darling."

It's said, and the response is quick and rewarding.

"Good night, darling. Sleep well."

"And you. Come safely on Friday."

She dances around the kitchen then, whirling her robe, celebrating. He does care. That's reason enough to justify herself for infidelity and for abandoning Henry and everything. She's alive. Really and truly. Someone has recognized her at last. She feels it right down to her toes. Of course she won't die. That was yesterday. Forget it. It won't happen. It can't.

Can it? She stops dancing and feels menace hiding nearby, waiting to pounce. It can happen. It will, unless she stops it. But she's alive now. Finally able to influence events. If living is going to be lovely, if she can recoup the losses of her life, she can slip away and have the operation after all and be reborn. Easy. She's quite young . . . there could be years and years. She mustn't forget to thank Edith for encouraging her. Perhaps she'll be able to do some encouraging herself. Of course she had wanted to die . . . it was a natural consequence of her depressed state after a depressed life that led her to assume there was no way of changing her condition. Well. Now it is changed. Her assumption was mistaken. What's forty-two? As good an age for a beginning as twenty-four.

Hannah is high, high. She can afford to be generous. She will telephone Henry and put his dutiful fears at rest, then he can enjoy himself too. One way or the other, she's going to set him free: which way is really not his concern. He is going to be free, and if he has any life-force at all, he'll invest his liberty and get a solid return on it. They may even end as loving friends. How satisfactory. How mature.

So she rings Henry and hurts his feelings, careless, self-centered, because the separation is turning out to be more upsetting to Henry even than the armed truce that preceded it. He's accustomed to good, unobtrusive housekeeping and finds to his surprise that dust accumulates on surfaces, the laundry box doesn't magically process clean shirts and underwear, meals have to be thought about before, during, and after consumption. It's a lot to do. Boring and fraught with complication. He's already very tired of boiled eggs, and the cooker's looking dirty. Germ traps everywhere. All these nasty discoveries relate to the absence of Hannah. No one called hullo when he came home on Monday. No one had wiped the rim of beard dust from the washbasin. She's only been gone a couple of days. How long will the house hold together? The toilet roll is running out. It's never been Henry's function to think about such things. And he finds he would be glad to think of them if, as a recompense, he had a familiar presence in the house, a head to talk to that knew his story. Hannah.

He begins to think she was right to go away, because now he's missing her and worrying about her and wants her back and is willing to reconstruct their joint existence on a different basis.

If he can explain this to her, then he's certain she'll meet him halfway and it can all be sorted out. Surely she must be missing him too? Twenty years. Nearly half of each of their lives. Doesn't time count for anything? He's so relieved when she phones, so ready to assure her that her tactics have worked, so ready to plead guilty to neglect of her spirit and to expiate his fault.

But she sounds strange, impatient with his questions.

"I'm absolutely fine, Henry. It's a very nice place."

"Are you sure you're all right? Hannah, I'm very worried . . . really. The house isn't the same without you . . . the doctor phoned . . ."

"Oh Henry. Please don't fuss. I told you, I'm fine."

"Have you thought at all about . . ."

"Do stop picking at me, Henry. I am thinking. But I'm rather enjoying the change too. It's so different . . ."

"Away from me, you mean." He's quick to be hurt and her answering silence is a fraction too long.

"I don't want to quarrel." She's curt because she's annoyed with him for being exact and breathing a smear of reality on her wonderful crystal bubble.

"No, no. Of course not." He rushes to placate her and tries to retrieve her good humor with a change of subject. "What are you doing with yourself?"

"Oh, this and that. I've got some work to do for David and I'm reading a bit, and walking and things."

The implicit lie trips easily off her tongue and leaves a foul taste in her mouth. Henry sounds so much of home and safety, so clean, any deviousness in his remarks is so glaringly easy to spot and is only there at all because he's worried. And there she is, an adulteress, feeling no guilt for the adultery but hating herself for her dishonesty and cowardice. If she isn't ashamed or guilt-ridden, why is she anxious to make little of David's visit?

138

"Oh, I see. Well, that's good, keeping busy. Hannah . . ." He can't not mention it again. "Hannah, look. You really do have to have the operation. You can't simply die . . . I don't think it's allowed, even."

Oh, Henry. The wrongest thing to say.

Hannah freezes. Who is it will not allow it? The state? How dare it? And how can it? Will she be taken by force, in a strait-jacket? Court orders, newspaper headlines . . . *Middle-Aged Housewife Preserved for Old Age.*

"I'll talk to you again in a day or two, Henry."

"Hannah, please . . ."

"Good-bye."

Now her bubble is crazed all over with cracks. She shouldn't have spoken with Henry tonight. Her hold on new life was still too tenuous. It would have been much wiser to wait until she had established herself more securely. Now she finds it doesn't help to murmur her mantra. She can't call up David's face. She shivers with embarrassment at the memory of her abandon, makes a grimace of distaste at the thought of the greed of her mouth for his body. And she can't even imagine his face. He's just some strange man.

She runs away to bed, though it's still very early, curls up tightly, screws up her eyes like a child, and waits for sleep.

It won't come. Back in a morass of confusion, worse than before she thought she'd escaped it, Hannah longs for authority. Someone to take all these dreadful, tangled loose ends, unpick the knots, and roll them into a neat little figure-eight hank. Mother. She never threw away bits of string or cut string off parcels with scissors. Every knot, no matter how tight, would be untied by those blunt, clean, scissor-cut nails with their overgrown cuticles and stowed away in a kitchen drawer. Buying new string is immoral.

Discipline. Rules of conduct. Why am I not like you, Mother? You tried, but it didn't take. Not a happy life, yours. Who said it had to be happy? But a course set and followed as circumstances permitted. Satisfaction. It's a kind of happiness.

Hannah's head aches, her back aches. What if David arrived now? Or Henry? Or David and Henry? Would she know what to do? Would she turn to one or the other or neither? If the stirring up of the past weeks counts for anything, surely it ought to be neither?

But now, this moment, what can she do to escape the immediate turmoil?

She gets up again and, hating the red robe, wraps herself in a blanket and creeps down the stairs. The ache in her back persists, distracting her attention to itself and from her thoughts, but the thoughts pull against it and Hannah feels miserably unwell. She makes tea in the kitchen and huddles in a corner under her blanket, holding her cup in both hands like a survivor of a shipwreck.

Henry is dutiful . . . that is indisputable, and she has considered going back to him as an easy option. He would look after her even now, out of a sense of duty, and she has considered that unacceptable for her and weak of him. But she begins to find similarity between Henry's unswerving observance of what he sees as his duty and her mother's rigid adherence to her principles. Lacking her mother, isn't Henry a very good substitute? Yes, he is. And like her mother a totally reliable support. Admirable. And like her mother totally unable to abdicate the role of supporter when the need no longer exists.

Hannah has come full circle. Henry is too supportive. Her mother was too supportive. Hannah's spiritual muscles were held in such tight corseting that they had no exercise at all and atrophied. She rearrives at her earlier conclusion. It has to be her doing, by herself. She has to identify herself. But this time, she's more tired, and the spiritual muscles are sore from the exercising they've started on. And her back aches.

But she'll do it. She'll do the research for David . . . that commits her to nothing and is in any case an interesting way to pass time. She'll meet new people and they'll meet new Hannah. Fresh encounters. And David?

"Misconduct." Mrs. Owen's mouth is sullied by the word. "Being Intimate. Disgraceful."

David. His face is there, in focus.

"Good night, darling. Sleep well."

She reaches under the blanket to rub at the ache in her back and the motion of her hand reminds her. His hands, his mouth. Kisses that first shocked, then transported her. At her age. She's waited all this time. It's right she should have something in exchange for her time. Did she not contribute her share to her mother's satisfaction and Henry's duty? They needed an object to support and she was it.

She shrugs the blanket more snugly around her, unhooks the phone, and dials Edith's number.

"Hullo, Edith. It's me, Hannah."

"How are you?"

"Fine. You?"

"The same." Edith gives a dry laugh.

"Look, I'm going to have a day in London on Thursday. Would you like to go up too and we could have lunch?"

"Oh? Bored?"

"No, it's not that. I need some things. Well, will you come?"

"Thursday? Well, all right. Yes. Where shall we meet?"

The arrangements are made quickly. Hannah's not clear why she's asked Edith to meet her, but it has something to do with David and with a decision finally reached not to hold back from anything involvement with him may bring.

Maybe it's a hand to hold when she steps into the water that she wants from Edith.

That's that, then, she says to herself and goes back to bed and sleeps.

Sixteen

Hannah sleeps late on Wednesday, but it doesn't matter. She's in no hurry, though there's plenty to do. David gave her a line of inquiry to follow in the village, and it must be done today, because tomorrow she's going to meet Edith, and the day after David will be back. If there weren't these specified claims on her time, it would be very easy and terribly tempting to slip into sluttishness, lying in bed to all hours and then slopping about without bothering to dress or brush her hair. It's an unexpected facet of the new situation: having neither Mother requiring her to be occupied nor Henry expecting her to be occupied. Can it be that it's her nature not to be occupied? She's never thought herself lazy, slovenly, but then she's only in the early stages of acquaintanceship with herself. She'd rather not discover herself to be a sloven, so she persuades herself out of bed and insists on dressing properly before she allows herself downstairs for breakfast. Her back aches. It's more evident than it used to be . . . probably unaccustomed activity with David has aggravated it, she thinks, and only then, quite calmly, does she realize that it has nothing to do with David.

It's the beginning of corruption, and it can only get worse.

Now she'll have to make a firm decision. Saturday. After

David's been again, on Saturday she'll decide. If she's going to have the operation after all, it will have to be soon, and it will be because there's a realizable prospect of a continuing present—and a future. And that, she hopes, will be clarified after Friday, after seeing David again without the blurring effects of the first delirium.

She takes a couple of aspirins and goes out. She feels timid about asking questions of strangers: instigating conversations doesn't seem natural to her, but she finds that people are willing to talk and recall long-gone times with nostalgia. That gives her pause. They seem to feel no hostility in recollection, no bitterness for things lost.

The baker who was kind to her on her first morning had a grandfather who was coachman and later chauffeur at the Big House. He lived in an estate house, his wife talked babies with the squire's wife and had laid out the squire when he died.

"It weren't no task for strangers, you see, without a proper understanding of what kind of man he'd been."

The mother of the post office lady had been in service at the Big House.

"Lovely linen they gave me when I married. A fine present."

The old man who apparently lives on the settle behind the door at the pub used to be gardener at the Big House. The squire used to say that his green fingers made the roses bloom better than any newfangled chemicals.

"And now?" Hannah asks the landlord. "Is it the same now? Does everyone still have a connection with the Big House?"

"No. It's one of those Management Studies Centers now, and the land's leased out. Pity though. The family had been part of the village for a couple of hundred years and more. It loosens the soil all around when roots that deep are pulled up, if you see what I mean."

Hannah sees. She sees that contentment with the order of things is given as natural to some. That is enviable, to be given contentment. But if you're not given it, then surely you must not settle for discontent without question? Surely contentment can be sought?

She asks and listens all morning. All afternoon, she makes copious notes, all day she keeps very busy so that she can get her allotted task finished and not have time to slide into the mudpool of ifs and buts where she has been trying to find her depth for too long now. At the end of the day, satisfaction is her reward. For hours at a stretch, she hasn't thought about herself at all and it is wonderfully restoring. She's tired by evening. Properly tired, not from running around and around in a treadmill, getting nowhere except back to where she started from, but from decent activity. She thanks David sincerely for insisting that she work.

So, having earned it, she sleeps soundly, and before she sleeps her mind is filled with other people, real lives, instead of useless conjecture about herself and her state.

The sense of being a functioning person remains when she wakes. Perhaps if she'd found work to do, instead of whipping herself into being a frightfully good but resentful house-keeper, she would have been an altogether more laudable person. Who couldn't be a frightfully good housekeeper if they'd devoted as much time and energy to it as she has?

Another futile Perhaps.

No more If Onlys. London and Edith are waiting, and before Edith, Hannah has secret, important things to do. Friday is very significant. There are preparations to be made.

She arrives on Thursday by train and bus and tube at a shop she has identified from Cyril's magazines.

Aladdin's Cave, hung with silks and satins, scented, twilit, erotic. Hannah is transported, and she slides her fingers over the beautiful fabrics, murmurs in delight over colors and textures, the atmosphere of commitment to sensuality takes hold of her and her thoughts turn to David and tomorrow. Will he like this? Will that make him smile, even as his breath grows short, will these amuse him, make him chuckle even as his eyes half close? Excitement begins to throb in Hannah, and her lips are dry. She licks them and is reminded of David's tongue, touching, flickering, a snake. No distaste now, no embarrassment. Let tomorrow, which means David, come quickly. This day must be filled, so that it can hurry away and bring tomorrow, and tomorrow, please, will bring Monday again, but without the preliminary, punishing uncertainty.

After Aladdin's Cave, there's food and wine to see to, sensual wonders wrapped in grease-proof paper, dreams and seasons in polythene bags, waiting to be let out. She hurries back to the station in a taxi to deposit her treasures. There are too many to carry but also she doesn't want to be bothered by curiosity from Edith.

Edith sails into the restaurant in a tremendous cape and a complicated turban. Heads turn and Edith, Hannah sees, accepts majestically what she identifies as admiration and Hannah feels is likelier to be stunned surprise. Edith's cape, thrust forward by bosom and falling in a straight line from there, makes her appear vast. Her head, confined in the turban, is by contrast very small. How has all the hair been accommodated? Hannah puzzles.

"You look remarkably well," Edith says after a searching look at Hannah. "The air must suit you."

Hannah is intrigued to find that she feels close to Edith, yet only that one instance of intimacy really links them. Can acquaintance become friendship because of one incident of intimacy? She smiles slyly, thinking of David.

"What are you snickering about?" Edith asks, pulling off her gloves, satisfied with her entrance.

"Nothing. Really. I'm glad to see you, Edith. How are you?"

"Well"—Edith settles herself and leans forward across the little table—"it has been a very odd sort of week. You seem to have started something."

"I have? What do you mean?"

"Everybody's unsettled, I think you'd call it. I mean, wives just don't simply go away, not our sort of wives. And you did. The girls are talking again about your little performance at my house that day . . . incidentally, that car that sparked it off was Christine's, out of petrol. That was why no one recognized it, because she was new. Janet's having kittens because George says he wants to give up his job and be a market gardener. He's completely serious, she says, and can you imagine

Janet digging potatoes out of frozen ground at dawn? To say nothing of his pension rights. And Cyril keeps giving me funny looks and asking if I feel all right. Naturally, dear, I haven't told him a word of what you told me."

Hannah is confident that's true.

"I'm sorry," she says. "I didn't mean to shake the foundations."

"Of course you did. That's exactly what you meant." Edith is matter-of-fact.

Hannah reflects.

"Yes," she agrees. "I suppose I did. But I didn't realize how much was built on them."

They order lunch and chat about shops while they're served.

"Why did you suggest meeting?" Edith asks. "We've never done it before."

"Everything's changed, isn't it? I don't want to bring things up that you'd rather not have mentioned, but you're the only one apart from Henry who knows about me, and you confided a little in me, so I'm afraid I'm making use of you. Looking for a friend, a woman friend."

"All right. That's fine. You haven't changed your mind during your retreat?"

Hannah chews her lip and plays with a pellet of bread.

"I'm not sure. I think I may be changing it."

Edith eyes her shrewdly.

"The isolation? Counted your blessings?"

"No."

"Henry?"

"No."

"Ah."

"What do you mean, 'Ah'?"

"Hannah, do please be very, very careful." Edith for once looks uneasy, unsure of herself. She takes a sip of wine and Hannah has guessed that something concerning David's visit to her is about to be said. She's not going to help Edith, though she feels a cold lump of guilt because Christine has entered the scene, silently. But it's remarkably easy to subdue the guilt and replace it with warm anticipation and turn her mind firmly to satin knickers securely and anonymously waiting at the station left-luggage office. Edith says, "Look, I've gossiped plenty in my time, I admit. But I've seen a fair bit of Christine lately, and bearing in mind what she's told me, and that David is working with you, well, if I put two and two together correctly, he may have something to do with your change of heart."

She waits for help. Hannah remains silent. Edith frowns, then plows on. "He's a . . ." and stops, unable to find the right word. "He plays games. He's dangerous. Faithless."

Hannah exclaims. Such an unexpected word. Archaic. And a flash of anger runs through her too, because Edith is speaking like an aunt. She, Hannah, is a grown-up woman herself, she's perfectly able to handle her own affairs, and anyway, no one is to criticize David.

"He comes and goes," Edith wades on. "They're not married because he insists he has to be free to come and go. He's always come back so far. She longs to be married . . . she works desperately hard at that flat calm of hers. It's the only way she knows to keep him . . . to let him go when he wants . . . and pray he'll be back. Everything they have is on his terms. She accepts that and bends with it."

For a moment, the old Edith shows.

"I wouldn't have it, I can tell you. He'd come back and find he'd overplayed his hand and lost the game."

Then she softens again.

"Oh, I don't know. Didn't I do a version of the same thing? Who am I to talk?"

Hannah feels she has to say something. It's clear Edith truly has her welfare at heart.

"I've been doing some work for him. It was a revelation to me, the enjoyableness of work. I really, actively enjoyed it. And I enjoyed his company too."

A shade of defiance there. Hannah is not going entirely to forswear herself.

"Don't worry, Edith. It's sweet of you to be concerned . . . I do appreciate it . . . but there's no need."

She stops there, carefully not going into details or leaving loopholes for questions. Poor Christine. But she's young, and she's deliberately chosen her way, not had it thrust on her. Hannah's need is greater now, and Christine shall have him back later, after Hannah's turn. If it weren't her, it would be some other woman who wouldn't care for him nearly as well.

But Hannah is vexed nevertheless. She doesn't want to think about endings. All I'm asking for, she pleads with herself, is the now of it. I'll think about the rest another time, but no one is going to be hurt.

"Well, if you're sure . . ." Edith isn't convinced and has only unconfirmed guesswork to go on.

"Tell me about Cyril." Hannah diverts the current.

"Hmm. He's no fool. I don't think Henry's told him anything explicit, but he's quite able to pick up clues. He's probably guessed at something not too far from the truth. He's been very sweet, as a matter of fact. Almost uxorious, as if he quite likes me."

"Oh good." Hannah is genuinely delighted. She wants happiness for everyone, conveniently overlooking Christine. "I am glad. Isn't that lovely? Who knows, it may . . ."

Edith looks bleak.

"I'm not sure I know how I feel anymore. I hadn't thought about it for ages till the day when you shook me up. It had become such a habit, the way we were. I don't know if I want all the effort of changes. I feel tired. Honestly, I think I ought to get away too and see it from a distance. Do you know, I didn't even realize how different he looks now from the way he was. Or me. I've had my hair cut."

"What!" Hannah's exclamation causes heads to turn.

Edith flushes, quite shy.

"New hat." She motions. "Didn't you notice?"

"Yes, of course. But I thought you must have pinned your hair flat. What does Cyril think?"

"He says it makes me look younger. Henry pretended not to notice, as if I'd had a nasty accident."

Hannah laughs.

"I wish Henry would . . . oh dear, I wish I knew the an-

148

swers. I'm thinking about the operation. I'll decide one way or the other in a day or two. You see, doing a job, for the very first time, has made me think that probably a great deal of my dissatisfaction has been my own fault. I could have been much more active about doing something with myself, rather than staying at home, bemoaning my fate, and making a scapegoat of Henry. He didn't ever want me to work, but that needn't have been insurmountable. I know it's rather late in the day to start thinking in terms of a career, but there must be something I could do, don't you think?"

"Like what?" Edith asks flatly.

Hannah was eager when she spoke, hopeful. A spark had ignited spontaneously in her. Equally suddenly, it's extinguished and she deflates.

"Like what, indeed," she echoes.

Edith repents of her realism.

"No, look," she tries to recant. "There are all sorts of openings for a mature woman. You've brought up children. You can cope with things. You're quite young . . ." she trails off, disheartened.

"Let's have brandy with our coffee," Hannah suggests brightly. "We might as well do things with a bit of style."

The brandy after their half bottle of wine jollies them up, and Edith says out of the blue, with a conspiratorial leer, "Actually, I could fancy David. Couldn't you, honestly?"

Hannah studies her brandy, and in its amber she sees the fox head, the amber hair. She smiles wickedly.

"Now you mention it, yes, I could."

"He's not a bit like Cyril. Or Henry."

"Not a bit." Hannah means more than Edith does.

"I wonder what he's like," Edith stage whispers. "You know . . . what he's *Like.*"

"I wonder," says Hannah and smothers a giggle. She's feeling quite lightheaded. Edith signals the waiter for more brandy and, refueled, pursues the topic.

"Have you ever? With anyone other than Henry? Girls do nowadays, but it was different, wasn't it? It wasn't the same for us."

149

"No, I haven't." Hannah doesn't consider it a lie because what she did with Henry wasn't the same thing at all as what she did with David. "I nearly might have, if you see what I mean, when I was seventeen, with a Frenchman."

"Oh, a Frenchman. But no, really?"

Hannah shakes her head.

"Have you?"

Edith's gaiety turns maudlin.

"Sort of. In a way. I thought I could punish Cyril for one of his little escapades. In the event, the only one who got punished was me."

"Go on," Hannah prompts.

"Well. There was a girl in his office that Cyril was chasing. You know, built like a boy with no figure at all." Edith adjusts her bosom automatically. "And he was quite besotted. And in the office as well was this rather divine-looking young man. I was about thirty-five and feeling very low, you know, doing the cooking and the cleaning and the washing, all to keep Cyril clean and healthy for this chit of a girl to reap the benefit. Because I certainly wasn't reaping any. Well, I went to great lengths to organize this Apollo to the house one evening when I knew Cyril was out with the girl, and I did the whole bit. Sexy dress, dim lights, loaded drinks. And he turned out to be as queer as a coot. Only I didn't find out till we were actually in bed and he cried, real tears, and said he wanted to be straight and he'd thought he'd be able to manage it with someone who reminded him of his mother."

A long pause. Hannah and Edith stare at each other, wide-eyed, then explode into laughter, sending a spray of brandy across the table.

"Oh dear," Hannah gasps, mopping her eyes. "Oh Edith, how marvelously ghastly. But at least it was an experience."

"Hmm," says Edith, composing herself and smiling bitterly, "only nearly. And guaranteed to humiliate me out of risking it again. I never will now, I suppose. Who'd fancy me, at my age?"

"Cyril?"

That pulls Edith up short and a very serious look comes over her face.

"I'd have to give that some more thought," she says, beginning to pull on her gloves. "You might be right. Or perhaps I'm past it. Though I'm not sure. What have I got to lose, anyway?"

Immediately, Hannah wants to be off. Edith too. Hannah wants to hurry back to Suffolk, where her life is. She doesn't want to lose that. Edith wants to go home and have another look at Cyril.

They part casually, too interlocked now to bother with their usual fulsome leave-taking.

"Shall I tell Henry we've met?"

"Why not? I'm not in hiding. Tell him I'll phone."

"Right. Well . . . whatever you're doing, take care."

"Give my love to Cyril."

"Yes. Well. Good-bye then. Keep in touch."

"Of course."

They go their separate ways, and Hannah frets because the journey takes time and there's nothing she can do but sit and wait to arrive, and while she's waiting she's prey to realism. What if David doesn't come? All sorts of things might prevent him. Pressure of other work. Car trouble. Lack of interest. Even, ultimate horror, direct avoidance of her. She could have become an exasperating complication in his life. She can just imagine how it could seem to him . . . a menopausal woman frantically taking a last-ditch stand against encroaching age and making herself ridiculous in the process, an embarrassing joke.

Oh no. He didn't feel that on Monday. He doesn't. He said he was drawn to her. That was explicit. No, it will be all right. She's not ridiculous. He has regard for dignity.

The phone is ringing when she lets herself into the cottage and she spills her packages on the table. She's afraid it's Henry, with a plaintive voice casting a blight on her evening, and briefly considers not answering, but that would only postpone him, so she lifts the phone and says hello in a carefully neutral tone.

"Darling. Where have you been?"

It's David, and the sudden shock of joy takes Hannah unawares.

"Oh David, it's you. Oh darling, darling, how lovely!" She says it without thinking.

"I miss you," he says, his voice making her shake. This is me, talking to my lover. Edith doesn't know how he looks, how he sounds. Edith only knows the social envelope. I know. He's my lover and my love.

"Oh David, I miss you too. I think about you all the time."

"Can I stay tomorrow?" He's asking. Actually asking.

"Come as quickly as you can and stay forever."

How easily she slips into the way of love, the undefended honesty.

"What are you wearing?"

She laughs.

"My coat. I've just this moment come in. I've been to London."

"Whatever for?"

"Wait and see. I had lunch with Edith."

"Oh. How did that go?"

"Quite well. We mentioned you in conversation."

"I don't think Edith approves of me."

Why does he say that? Is that a defiant or a defensive note?

"I approve of you. And I'm dying to see you."

"Shall I tell you what we're going to do tomorrow?"

He begins to itemize the ways he'll caress her, to specify kisses and embraces, and Hannah shivers with awful lust. Her mouth is dry and her knees shake.

"Stop, darling. I can't bear it."

He laughs, but not in a conquering way. More sharing.

"Good night, darling. Sleep well."

"Good night. David?"

"Yes?"

She wants to say she loves him, but something holds her back. The enormity of it, some residue of self-protection, a pinprick of conscience.

"Drive carefully. Come safely."

She sits in the kitchen, still in her coat, letting the memory of his words flow over her like honey, and scraping at the honey with a sharp spoon comes Edith's voice . . . "Faithless," and an image of Christine, silently waiting in an empty house, and Henry in another empty house, stoically filling page after page of the book that will never be finished.

Don't look, God. There's no need for You to watch. With all You've got to keep an eye on, You could afford not to notice this. On a cosmic scale, it's so very small a sin. To me, it's the Great Adventure. And I'm not really sinning, not damaging anything that isn't broken already. All right, God? Fair's fair. You made me, so if there's fault, You've got to go shares in it.

She gets up, rubbing her back, and starts methodically unpacking her shopping. By the time the extravagant, delicious food has been put away and she turns to the small, soft packages, her conscience has been anesthetized. It's a dreadful nuisance, serves no useful purpose, it has to be put to sleep. She cannot allow herself to be weighed down by other people's destinies.

There's still Henry. She has to lay him to rest, too, before she can give herself up entirely to anticipation.

"Hullo, Henry. It's me."

"How are you? Edith phoned a little while ago."

"Fine. How are you? Are you managing all right?"

He gives a rueful laugh.

"I'm no cook."

"But I thought you'd eat out mostly." She really did.

"You know how I hate to eat out."

"It's quite safe, Henry, really."

"I know, I know. I've been spoiled, I suppose."

Goodness me. How true. How remarkable that he should say it. She feels concerned for him, but he really must be encouraged to make constructive use of this separation, as she is.

"Well, try one or two places. I'm sure you'll find somewhere nice."

"Mother phoned. She said she hadn't heard from you lately."

"Oh. What did you say?"

"That you'd got flu and couldn't phone because you'd lost your voice."

"Henry."

"I know. I should have told her the truth, or some of it."

"Yes, you should. Why didn't you?"

"She's getting on, Hannah. She'd be upset, and there's nothing to be gained by upsetting her at this point, is there? And she'd start agitating, and I can't face that at the moment."

"I do see, Henry, but she'll have to know sooner or later. Unless she dies before me."

"Hannah."

"Sorry."

"Edith said you'd told her all about it . . . and you'd said you might . . ."

"I'm thinking about it."

"It's the only reasonable . . ."

"Henry, stop picking."

Silence. Poor Henry. Hannah softens. It's easier to feel for him and to speak to him over the phone. His physical absence helps.

"I'll let you know definitely after the weekend."

"Joe said he might go and see you tomorrow or Saturday."

"*No.*" Hannah is appalled. She'd never thought of that.

"But you said . . ."

"I know I did. But not this weekend. Absolutely not. I want to be left alone to think things over. Tell him he mustn't come. Tell him, Henry."

"All right, all right. I'll tell him. Don't get upset."

"No. Well. I need peace and quiet to think."

"All right. Well, take care. I'll phone on Monday, shall I?"

"Yes. On Monday. Good-bye, Henry. Do try and eat properly."

"Yes. Good-bye."

Hannah, tight-lipped, opens a bottle of wine and drinks a glass. That's better. Much better. She pours another glassful and takes it upstairs with her, carrying too an armful of soft packages. She unwraps each package carefully, taking frequent sips of wine, and lays out over the bedroom a snail's trail of satin. A nightgown, a slither of mother-of-pearl, a negligee that conjures up locked compartments on huge international express trains rushing through the night, the so-long-awaited knickers, a suspender belt meant less for suspending than for defining hips and thighs. All these, and black stockings, silk.

She washes her hair, bathes with scented oil, and puts on the negligee. She wants it to absorb her shape and smell, so that it isn't a new garment but hers. She continues to sip wine and dines on olives and grapes, too committed to fantasy to be hungry.

At last she goes to bed, almost sleepwalking, drugged with wine and sensuality and the stillness of waiting without uncertainty for the fulfillment of hope.

Seventeen

Monday.

Now Friday and Saturday and Sunday have come and gone, and David has come and gone, and Hannah believes she sees her way ahead.

It's not the path that meanders around the gentle lower slopes of the mountain, with suds of harebells on either side and crossed by fairy grotto streams. Not the one sadly disappointed Hannah had hoped for and believed might lead home. It's the other one, that takes a turn and starts to climb, beyond the harebells, beyond the gentle slopes. It climbs and grows hard and is barren and crossed by biting wind. But at the top you can lean against the wind and it will support you while you look down and see the valley almost to its limits in each direction, from almost its beginning to almost its end.

Hannah, deluded by romanticism, believes the top to be attainable and herself strong enough to withstand the wind. How courageous. How carelessly she falls again into the well of error.

Friday came to pass and there was no flaw in it. A perfect achievement. What a pity, Hannah has been thinking, there isn't an award for the best lovers' meeting of the age. She would have had a ribbon to wear, a pretty rosette, so everyone would know there's something she's very, very good at.

Such communion of spirit, such blending, rich colors merging, tastes mingling, brandy and port. Unsurpassable. Every cliché revealing itself as a timeless truth. Soul mates, indisputably.

"The Friday of the world," David said. "Time out of time."

"The birthday of my life," said Hannah.

But he had to go late on Saturday and that was very terrible, but much safer. You don't try to follow the happy ending at the pantomime. Better to drop the curtain and go home with the gratification that you were there when happily-ever-after came true.

And the loneliness that filled the cottage like floodwater when he'd gone was very terrible, but Hannah can accept it as part of the package. She's being so mature, so realistic: David has commitments. His work, Christine. They have their place in his life, she has hers, and she believes now already that hers is inviolable.

David's marble detachment has been breached for, he swears, the first time. This love, this absolute, is as new to him as it is to her. He is bewildered by the way she has, in so short a space, become essential to him. So confident of his self, so secure in his ability to contain himself, allowing measured quotas here and there as it pleased him, he has not thought it possible that anyone, any woman, could cause him to fear the lack of her. He's not an inexperienced boy, he knows the magnitude of what he says. Whatever happens, and that is a gray and menacing cloud mass, whatever happens, he will never hurt her, never stop loving, now that so late in the day he has learned how.

All this he swears not on the treacherous ground of passion, but later, in the quiet, so that she believes him.

Hannah is proud. She is honored. She is humble. That she should be the one elected by Destiny or God or whatever to be David's love. All the waiting was worthwhile. The dreary years were leading to this, turning her into what she is, because she, the way she is, was what was planned for David.

She knows she is in love, a condition whose existence she has cynically doubted. But now it's so clear, there's no other

157

explanation for the way she feels, the incandescence in the air, the holiness that links her to him. Whether she loves him is a different matter. Being in love is sudden, loving takes time. They've talked long and unhurriedly, and Hannah has found much cause for love in David. If at this moment she's only in love, loving has been born.

But where can it lead?

In the night, as he slept and she lay awake, the question obtruded itself. Where can they go from here? And the answer came back, clear and unequivocal.

Nowhere.

It would be easy, wouldn't it? Dispatch Christine, eliminate Henry, and walk away together into the sunset while the music plays and the final titles come up on the screen. Easy. Dispose of communal property, break the anchor chains, fly away to paradise and eternal joy. No washing up, no ovens to clean, no rates to pay, no Mondays, only Fridays. Easy. Hannah looks at sleeping David, counts how few the lines on his face, and admits there is no future for them together, no projecting this rapture into a permanence where Mondays and ovens and rates are facts that clamor for attention. For a tiny while it would be marvelous, but, love apart, they have nothing in common, no history, and even though loving could grow between them, it's not a kindly loving she wants with him. That, had she been wiser years ago, she might have achieved with Henry. If it were what she wanted, Henry would have to be the one to share it. He deserves that much.

Honestly believing, in the deceptive, satisfied dark, that she is being rational, that she will be able to manipulate circumstances, that being in love now will be enough, Hannah yearns over David and renews her decision to let events take their course. She is not going to meddle with anything. Everything shall happen as it happens, in its own season without interference from her.

Somewhere along the way, she will tell David that she is dying and they will lovingly accept the natural term put to their being together. And after her death, David will be sad, bereft, grateful, and her memory will be perfect, a part of him for always. Hannah sheds a romantic tear and sees herself as a beautiful angel hovering over David, protecting and guiding him, and their love as a sphere of crystal, as priceless as a diamond and as indestructible.

So, after he's gone, she's not agitated. The moment he's out of sight, she begins to wait for his return, but quietly because the time will not hurry and the waiting is part of the joy of his arrival. He's brought her books: stalagmites of books and he wants her to read so that she can help him and to make up for what he calls gaping holes in her education. She's been lazy, he says, unproductive for years, coasting along on sweets and small talk instead of taking proper nourishment for her intelligence.

Obediently, she reads and begins to feel a stretching in her mind, at first quite uncomfortable. Often and often she looks up from the page and thinks, Oh what for? What a bore. I don't need to know all this, but more and more she's drawn back and involved until the moment comes when she reads an opinion and says, No. I don't agree with that, and then a little later produces cogent reasons for her nonagreement. This, thinks Hannah, is splendid. I have a mind of my own. I have opinions. My opinions may differ from others', but they are every bit as valid. So there, Henry.

Oh yes. Henry. He's not going to like it a bit when she tells him that she hasn't after all changed her mind. She shouldn't have even hinted to Edith that she was wavering. It will be harder now to tell Henry.

As if called into being by her thoughts of him, Henry phones.

"Well, Hannah. How are you? All set?"

"Yes, Henry. I . . ."

"I knew you'd see reason. I knew it. Once you'd got over the shock."

"Henry. Stop it. I haven't changed my mind. No operation."

Silence. She can imagine his face too clearly. It's a standard sort of face, a decent-Englishman face. She can imagine the incredulity, the bewilderment. She's not doing the decent thing. It grieves her to upset him. She's really very fond of him. She looks back at the turmoil of anger and fault-finding and blaming and can't recall the feeling of it. It was so long ago. Like a gathering boil, it spread its pain all around, because too inflamed to bear the lightest touch and slowly came to a head. Then in due time, the shining, red-hot throb shrank away to painlessness and the site of so irresistible an agony can only be identified by exploring fingers. A mark remains, but each day diminishes it and soon there will be no trace left. So Hannah has synthesized her feelings about her disputes with Henry. She respects his honor, accepts without argument the divergence in their views, recognizes the validity of the connections between them. A state exists. It doesn't have to be prodded and pulled anymore.

"Look, Henry. I know you don't understand. Can't you just accept my decision without understanding?"

"What makes you think I don't understand? Do you imagine I wouldn't like to opt out too? It's being made easy for you. I'd have to jump under a train or something."

Hannah is startled. And she's afraid Henry's going to start another argument. It's asking for trouble to squeeze the area of an extinct boil, there's no certainty it won't be provoked into erupting again. And more: what does he mean, opt out? That makes it seem a dereliction of duty, irresponsible, cowardly.

"Opt out? If there were any prospect of a worthwhile future, I'd take it, Henry. I'm not opting out. I'm trying to save us all a great deal of disturbance and distress. And to let you have your chance too."

She can't help letting a breath of righteousness creep in alongside the indignation. His answering pause gives her time to recognize and despise her own theatricality.

"We can't talk about it on the phone. I'll rearrange my appointments for tomorrow and drive down to see you. We've got to arrange ourselves once and for all."

Hannah doesn't want him to be in the cottage, sitting in the chair where David sits, making waves in her pond, but she has to agree that he's right. Once and for all. Then it should be plain sailing for the rest of her time. It will be a relief to have everything sorted and everyone knowing where he stands. Unconsciously sly, she doesn't count that David is to be left uninformed and Henry is not to know about David and Christine is not to know about Hannah.

"Yes, you're right. What time?"

"Before lunch, I should think. I'll have to organize a bit."

"Henry, I don't want to fight." Hannah is nervous.

"Neither do I. It's an indictment of both of us that you mention it. No fighting. Good night then, my dear."

"You've never called me that before."

"No. I've been thinking too, you know. You are dear to me."

Hannah is moved. Henry sounds strong. She's just hit him again and it rocked him, but it was only a momentary stagger. That's the way it is with Henry. He is what he seems. A man to lean on, a shelter in rough weather, his weakness that he needs too much to be leaned on, insists on giving protection when his charges would be better served by having to rely on their own strength.

"Thank you, Henry. I'll expect you tomorrow."

She puts the phone down and wonders why he didn't say that, like that, fifteen years ago. Because she had already stopped listening? Because he didn't think it needed saying in words? Because they had both been put by their parents into separate compartments of a driverless train and hadn't the wit or experience to notice the communication cord? Oh, it's sad. But it's the past. She's ready to look to the future and fill it with living. It's started already. Already she's filled some of the holes, already she's making up lost time. She can accomplish a lot more. The nightmare of realization has left her alone while she's been occupied and preoccupied with other things. If she keeps on being busy, she can hold it at bay, and at the end, she assumes, someone will give her something that will float her away easily. Not heroically aware like her mother, but isn't it something of an achievement to acknowledge that she doesn't have that kind of courage and to adjust accordingly?

She goes to bed and lies alone, thinking that things are falling into place. Chaos is ending and order is returning. How different an order from before, but how attractive order is of itself, once one has stared eyeball to eyeball at the alternative.

Only as she's falling asleep does she realize that David hasn't phoned during the evening. It snaps her awake.

Perhaps he's had an accident, or maybe he's ill. How can she find out? Impossible to endure not knowing. What if he died and no one saw any reason to tell her? Cold sweat breaks out on her forehead and she feels real fear. Why doesn't he drive to a phone box? He's working then? Yes, that could be it. He becomes totally absorbed when he's writing and he does have deadlines to meet. Hannah chews the edge of her sheet and forces herself into calm. He must have rung while she was talking to Henry. If he doesn't try again it's because he has a good reason. He'll call tomorrow. Tomorrow will come more quickly if she sleeps. She soothes herself with recollections of Friday and finally sleeps, tightly curled up, clutching the sheet.

And in the morning, early, David phones.

"Hullo, darling. Sleep well?"

"Eventually."

"Sorry I didn't call you. I meant to but I got very involved with a publisher over dinner. Couldn't get away, and then it was too late."

"I was worried."

"Oh come on, Hannah. Don't fuss."

She doesn't like that. He ought to be upset that he's worried her. He ought to fuss a bit. No, she's being silly and girlish.

"Well." She forces a laugh of sorts. "Never mind. When are you coming?"

"Friday?"

"Not till then? It seems ages away."

"Yes, it does. Too long." That's more like it. Hannah relaxes. "Tell you what, I'll reorganize. I'm up to my ears at the moment, but I must see you. How about Thursday?"

"It's sooner than Friday, darling. Yes, please."

"Right. Thursday. I'll ring before then of course. Take care, darling."

"David?"

"Yes?"

"I love you."

"That's marvelous to hear. See you Thursday. 'Bye."

An unsatisfactory conversation. Still, Thursday is only two days away and she has plenty to do. And Henry will be here before very long. She tidies up the cottage and goes to the village shop and prepares lunch. Henry will like that, appreciate it after such rude disruption of his eating habits . . . nothing exotic, a good, wholesome meal.

But none of the preparations can keep Hannah's mind off David.

A sense of impropriety makes her reluctant to phone him at home. She must suggest that they arrange some means for her to contact him somehow. She's too cut off, relying always on him to call her. It threatens her. He didn't say anything lovely this morning. He accepted her love, but didn't return it. She begins to feel hurt and tearful, and frustrated that there's no way she can speak to him and hear him reassure her. She'll be glad when Henry comes and occupies some of the time till the next phone call.

Henry said before lunch, and at eleven-thirty he arrives. He's lost some weight. Only a little over a week, but Hannah's sure he's thinner.

They kiss like cousins, on the cheek, and behave like cousins with a communal past and separate lives.

Hannah hurries to start lunch. She remembers thinking once before that it helps to have something legitimate to do with your hands. Henry is flatteringly pleased with the meal, but eats very little, and soon puts down his fork and begins.

"There's no point in putting this off, Hannah. It's why I came. I'm not browbeating you, or blaming you for anything, but I want you to have the operation, and after it, when you're properly fit, we'll consider what we should do about ourselves. I take note of what you say about lost opportunities

163

and second chances. I understand your feelings perfectly, but that's not the way life is. It's a romantic ideal. It doesn't really happen like that."

"Oh it does. Sometimes it does."

"Only often enough to prove the rule."

"You could have a second chance at living, Henry. Really you could."

"No. I don't want one. Nor do you, you've said. It was right to separate us for a while, to crystallize our ideas. I don't want any more chances. I don't want to find myself an old man with all my ambitions explored. You have to leave yourself a Maybe or a Perhaps. I might have been a good artist. I don't know. But I'm hanging on to the idea so that I can say to myself, I could have done this or that, instead of being left high and dry knowing I'd tried and failed. I'm a good dentist. And I might have been a good artist instead, if I'd had a chance to try. But I don't want the chance."

That's a very long speech for Henry. It's all prepared and pre-thought. And Hannah knows what he means. He means precisely what she means. Sinkingly she sees clearly that she has been trying to use him, to force a second chance on him as a justification for refusing one herself.

"Oh Henry," she sighs. "I wish I'd known you years ago."

Then they are both surprised, because she spoke without thinking and told the truth of it. Had they known each other, they would have adjusted their differing shapes while they were still malleable and gradually fitted together, interlocking.

He reaches out his hand to her.

"We could have a second try together," he says. "This could make all the difference we'd need. We're too old to go swanning off independently. Let's get you well and have another go, only this time knowing what we're doing. We've a great deal in common. That's a good foundation, wouldn't you say?"

How disturbingly his conclusions resemble her own. They do have a great deal in common. Background, twenty years, children, a history. And she and David have nothing except excitement in unreal isolation. David will expand her intellect, but she's already understood that that is not enough. It's not living in the world together.

All Henry has said is true, reasonable, caring. He sits there, so admirable, in his dark suit and white shirt, saying, "Lean on me. Let me do my duty because it's my justification for living. If you lean on me, you are supporting me."

It would mean giving up David at once, and David represents so much of what she's missed, froth, bubbles, pleasure for its own sake.

It would mean committing herself again to the role of wife. Henry promises a new start, new patterns, and means it, but realism is not dead in Hannah and she knows that before long Henry-and-Hannah will be living apart, side by side, reading their library books, dining with neighbors, passing their time.

Henry is not able to change. He may want to, he would try to, but it's not in his nature, and no person can be expected to change his nature. And this time Hannah, having knowingly chosen the role, would have to enter into it unreservedly. And that is against her nature.

She shakes her head . . . oh, she doesn't want to hurt this good man. She's ashamed that she hurts him. But their natures collide. No one's fault. It's just too late to do anything, they're both too formed now. And David, oh, David and excitement and glamour, feeling young and desirable, candles and wine and romance. Of course it's unreal, but must it be denied because of that? What a barren, cold world it would be, devoid of unreality. Dreams are a necessary part of life. Even Henry sees that. She won't again be selfish enough to suggest that she is removing herself in order to gratify him; that wasn't fair. But she still hopes a dream will find Henry, willy-nilly, and she is going to remove herself so that she doesn't risk outliving her dream.

All this she thinks, her hand resting in Henry's, and he waits, as if for anesthetic to take effect so that he can start drilling.

"I'm desperately sorry, Henry. I can't do it. I really think I would if I could. But I can't."

He's silent for a long while. Then he slides his hand from

under hers and gets up. His face is grave. They look at each other, searching for comprehension and finding some. They understand each other enough for mutual respect.

"There's no more to be said, then," says Henry.

"No."

"Do you want to come home now?"

"I'd rather stay here a little longer."

He nods.

"You can't stay indefinitely. You'll let me know when you want to come home?"

"I don't deserve that."

"You're my wife. It's your home. I'll fetch you whenever you say."

"Thank you, Henry."

Hannah can't believe this conversation is happening. It's too unlikely, herself and Henry calmly talking, without acrimony, on a subject too tremendous to measure.

"Good-bye, Hannah. I'll keep in touch. You're all right for money?"

"Yes, thank you. I'm very grateful." And sorry and ashamed and excited.

He smiles briefly but it's obvious he wants to go away, and there's nothing more to say and nothing more to be done. Hannah watches from the door as he walks to his car. A fine-looking man. His father would be proud of him. He's carried on the tradition and believed in it and kept faith with it. He's done it all the way he thought he should. Hannah loves him and bitterly regrets that he's been wasted on her as she was wasted on him.

After he's gone, she sits by the fireplace and cries.

Eighteen

The days accumulate. An hour lasts forever, but a week flashes by. Hannah lives quietly, not noticing time as she consumes it.

She finds herself moving slowly, often with a delicate tread because of the increasing ache in her back, disoriented, outside the lives around her. She goes for walks but tires easily and sits for long spells in the mild sunlight before making her way driftingly back to the cottage.

She knows the village now, especially the church, where she is irresistibly drawn to the weathered graves enclosed by a high wall. There's nothing morbid in her fascination. It's the old graves close to the church itself that she likes. The brash new ones with sharp-edged angels and rudely bright inscriptions don't appeal to her. The old ones are settled, everything worn smooth, the core of no piercing agony to anyone. Lives completed, far enough away to be seen in perspective, if anyone cares enough to look.

David is pleased with her and she's pleased with herself, gratified in an unexuberant way. Looking at buildings, looking at churches, is a gentle pastime, suitable to her mood. The durability of structures satisfies her, the house built for a family three centuries ago and still fit for its purpose, the church built without thought of doubt to last into an indeterminate future. No planned obsolescence. Continuity.

Hannah feels herself so transient, such a passer-through. Things that wear permanence like a warm coat impart their comfort to her, protect her from the cold wind.

And there's David. The world pivots around him. When he comes, the sleepwalking rhythm is transformed because all the time he isn't with her is waiting time. As soon as he is with her, she ceases to be transient, she's not passing through, she's charged with life, an idling engine suddenly engaged.

How well she understands now what Edith said about the rising of the sun, though she can't believe, except academically, that Edith or anyone could feel about Cyril or anyone what she feels for David.

And how does David feel about her?

She doesn't worry or wonder about that anymore. If he didn't care, he wouldn't come. He wouldn't phone at the beginning and ending of every day. He wouldn't tell her he loves her or bring her tiny treasures . . . a bunch of buttercups, a lucky charm. He doesn't have to do any of these things. The series of articles is long since finished, but still he comes, daily he assures her of love.

The monstrous uncertainty of the beginning is funny now. Hannah recalls how she squirmed that first evening. She remembers doing it, but can't remember how it felt. Her situation is guiltless. She is simply following her nature, so grateful that she found it and had the time and opportunity to nurture it that she's reached a state of stillness. Nothing to struggle against, no restraints, no tension. She speaks fondly to Henry quite often, able to care about him openly. Her separation from Henry has nothing to do with David. Nothing is David's fault. Nothing any longer is anybody's fault. No one robbed anyone. Things are as they are and will come to their destined conclusion. Even Christine doesn't trouble Hannah, even the thought of how much more of his time she has than Hannah has. Christine has lost reality.

It's the happiest time for Hannah. The summer's coming and she has everything she wants. Tranquil solitude, thrilling companionship, honest goodwill toward Henry, both her mind and her body being used for their purpose.

There is the pain in her back, which is very uncomfortable at times and never quite goes away now, and there are other indications of the disease gaining ground. She's getting very thin and very tired, and if she had to work or if David were with her more often, it would be a major effort to keep going, but none of it seems to matter very much. If this is the price of the treasures she's gathered, she's willing to pay without complaint.

Vaguely, she still regrets not having made an occupation for herself a long time ago, vaguely she still resents the waste, but everything's vague. Nothing has a keen edge except David. She never even thinks now of the ending. It will come, she knows, but vaguely. She will care, she supposes, but not fiercely, because by then she will be drifting away on a pain-killing ebb-flow. Someone will have taken charge, it won't be up to her. The someone doesn't have a face, but he has a Henry-like capacity for taking charge. She doesn't see this as an abnegation of the autonomy she made an issue of, but rather as a reasonable acceptance of her weakness as she's defined it.

Meanwhile she's content with the way things are. She's living under her own steam, autonomously, she's been honest with and about Henry, she's contributed to an artistic venture, she's released her body from its moral and physical inhibitions. Not bad. Rather good, really.

And passion. Anger and ambition and regret and love and lust. She's learned a bit about passion. Lost time accounted for. Experience brought up to date in some measure. It's all worth the price. And at the finish, a dignified exit. What more could a woman of her age ask? No one's going to have to clean up messes after her, or suppress guilty loathing of her old-woman's needs, or jollily lie about how pretty her sparse gray hair is.

But so much creaminess is troubling in itself. Now and again, when she can't sleep, or when she's too tired to read, Mrs. Owen comes close and hints darkly in that sarcastic, throwaway tone she used to disguise her love and concern, "A fool at forty is a fool indeed." And Hannah will nod, agreeing. How can she be sitting here so peaceful, hands idle, body decaying, life withdrawing, and nothing to complain about?

Hannah is in the kitchen one morning, five weeks into the rest of the rest of her life, contentedly sipping coffee, reading her book, a hot-water bottle lodged into the belt of her dressing gown. Breakfast. Leisurely, pleasurable. It's Tuesday. Before she's finished her coffee, David will phone and they'll chat, about nothing really.

All the anecdotes have been told; he knows about Mrs. Owen, and Mr. Owen, and Henry, and the boys. He knows about the tedious humiliations of being a Good Woman, about the decision to reshape her life. He doesn't know about the cancer, not yet. Hannah knows which school he went to and the course of his career and a thousand stories of people he's met and interesting or important events. She hasn't chosen to recognize the big empty holes he's left in the telling of himself.

She has all she needs. Why insist on more? Their conversations are repetitive, but they flow like sweet oil. She tells him she loves him and what they'll have for dinner. He tells her he loves her and what they'll do together. It's enough. Even when twice in the last ten days he hasn't been able to come as arranged, it was very disappointing, but not more. No doubt or anxiety attaches to him.

She's absorbed by what she's reading. It's a collection of imaginary interviews with great architects of the past and two of them are by David. It gives an extra dimension to something she'd find interesting anyway. She reads on to the end of the interview and glances at her watch and feels the first stirring of alarm. It's past his usual time, well past. What can have happened to him? However busy he is, since that dreadful time when he failed to call, he's always found a moment between nine and nine-thirty. Even if it's literally a one-minute call. So what's wrong? Perhaps he's had an accident . . . he's dead, or hideously injured, unconscious in the wreck of his car . . . no. No. No. It's probably just her watch. She switches on the radio just in time for a ten-o'clock time signal. It has to be the phone itself then. She can't be without a phone . . . it's her necessary link with David. It's a panicking thought that she might be out of touch with him, she can't, cannot, be without a phone. She must check on it, that's what she must do, check on it at once. But if it's not out of order after all, he might ring while she's talking to the Exchange. She'll wait for a few minutes. Be sensible. Stop being so neurotic. She waits ten minutes, staring at the instrument, beseeching it to ring, but it stares insolently back at her, silent. She picks it up gingerly and barely waits for the normal dialing tone to sound before she slams it down again.

Seriously worried now, she scurries upstairs and dresses in a rush to be ready for some unimagined emergency and hurries back to the kitchen.

What's happened? Something's happened. Hannah begins to feel sick. Time goes by, drip by drip.

By midday she's frantic, but afraid to move from the phone. He's coming tomorrow, she ought to shop, clean up, arrange flowers, wash her hair. But she dares not leave the kitchen.

Silly, she rebukes herself. Overreacting. There's the simplest explanation. I'll laugh when he tells me.

Only she's not laughing now. She's frightened. By midafternoon she's reached the limit of her endurance, picks up the phone and dials his number. It rings twice, then Christine's voice, "Hullo?"

Hannah can't speak.

"Hullo?" Christine again, calm, pleasant, not worried. There's no disaster. "Hullo? David, I think we've got an anonymous call."

And then David's voice faintly, cheerfully, "Say something rude. Give them a thrill."

Hannah slams the receiver back on the rest and sits at the table, feeling sick. She's hot and cold, sweating and trembling. He's there. So why? Why didn't he, doesn't he? She stays where she is, noticing the sweat, noticing the nastiness of her reaction, observing a middle-aged woman suffering over the lack of a phone call from a young man. When she looks at her watch again, over an hour has gone by and she's cold and ill. She's eaten nothing since her long-ago, happy breakfast, and it's been a long, terrible day. Calmly she gets up from the table and makes herself some tea and takes it into the living room. The breakfast debris, unappetizing and slovenly, is left. It doesn't matter. Then the phone rings. She drifts back to the kitchen and answers it coolly, feeling nothing.

"Darling," he says. "What a day. How are you?"

"Fine. You?"

"Surviving. My feet haven't touched the ground. Where have you been?"

"Here of course."

"I rang and rang."

"No one's rung all day." She can't help a tremor in her voice as the stunned calm begins to crack.

"Darling. There must be a fault on the line. Poor love. Look . . . tomorrow . . . something's come up. You remember I told you about a person in Cambridge who says he's in his third incarnation?"

Hannah remembers. She remembers it didn't seem David's cup of tea at all, and he laughed and said he had better things to do than chase mad old ladies. Now it's a man . . .

"I've contacted him and arranged to meet him. But tomorrow's the only evening he can manage."

"Oh, but David . . ." Hannah's eyes fill with tears. She'd rather he didn't say more, no explanations, too elaborate . . . they breed suspicion and she suspects him of nothing.

"I know, darling, I know. But I have to make a living." He laughs lightly. "Still, first things first. I must see you. I'll take the long way around and drop in on my way."

"But it's Wednesday."

"Hannah." A warning edge in his voice now.

"I'm sorry, I'm sorry. Of course you have to go. I'll see you tomorrow then?"

"Only for a minute, I'm afraid. Take care. Great to hear you. 'Bye, darling."

"Good-bye," she says faintly, wanting to scream, If it's great to hear me, why didn't you call? Why? Tell me. Explain.

She can't read. She can't listen to the radio. She can't do anything. He didn't say "I love you." Not once. She goes to bed and curls up small, the pain in her back forgotten because of the sick ache in her chest. She seems not to sleep, but the hours pass thickly and she must have dozed because at last it's morning and she sits up in bed and the sun is streaming into the pretty room and she thinks, What a nonsense. What a silly drama to make over a missed phone call. She's ashamed of herself.

She tosses her head in embarrassment at her behavior, autonomous, independent lady, and gets up and has a bath and listens for the phone.

At nine-twenty, when she's in the kitchen, it rings. She waits and lets it ring four times before she loses her nerve and snatches it up.

It's all right. He speaks lovingly. He'll come this evening. He sounds really sorry he can't stay. Of course she understands. He has to do his work. She must have misheard the details about the third incarnation.

There's so much to catch up on after yesterday that the day slides quickly by and at seven o'clock everything's ready. She's put out some wine and new bread and a beautiful pâté so that he can eat before driving on. Maybe he can even be enticed back from Cambridge after the interview.

The bread begins to harden. The pâté starts to dry. Nine o'clock, and Hannah moves from the window where she's stood for an hour and sits with her back to it in the dusk.

She's not thinking now, nor feeling. Her hands and feet are cold but it doesn't matter. When the car stops outside she stays where she is.

"Hannah. You're asleep." He's filling the room, putting on the light, alive, vigorous. "Sorry to be so late. I was held up. Can't stop, I'm afraid."

She stands up then, looks at him, puts her arms around his neck, leans nervelessly into him, so warm, so wonderfully familiar.

He kisses her obligingly, his tongue makes a cursory move into her mouth, then he puts her from him.

"Darling. Can't stop. I'm so late already. I promised them I'd be there . . ."

She doesn't say anything. He notices the bread and pâté.

"Pâté. Great. I'll take some to eat on the way."

As he helps himself and turns to go, Hannah finds her voice.

"David? Tomorrow?"

"Well . . ." he looks at her. "OK. Tomorrow. Dinner, yes?"

She smiles brilliantly.

"I'll make a special dinner."

"Marvelous. 'Bye, darling."

And he's gone. Five minutes? No, less. What's happening? Nothing. Nothing can happen. He loves her. He promised. Their love is real. Nothing can happen to that. Gold doesn't tarnish, diamonds don't crack. He'll never hurt her. It's just that he's involved in the world and hasn't had a moment to readjust to their private rhythm.

It's hard, very hard, to fill the time till tomorrow evening. Hannah reminds herself she must keep occupied and sits in the living room thinking lists of all the things she should and could do. The cottage needs a thorough clean. There's washing and ironing. Reading. Writing letters: she really must write to her mother-in-law and the boys. She sits there till she's too tired to do any of them, all the time wondering at the back of her mind why David's kiss was so uninvolved and brief. No excitement in it, no surge of lust at her closeness. Nothing. Polite it was. She expected to be kissed, so he did what was expected of him, without committing himself. A gentleman wouldn't embarrass a lady by rejecting her advance.

Every time the thought threatens to move to the forefront of her mind, she pushes it firmly away.

Tomorrow, it will be wonderful. Just like all the other times. Hannah trails up to bed at last and cuddles a hot-water bottle and wishes Mrs. Owen and Edith would learn to keep their mouths shut.

Nineteen

All night she dozes and wakes, worries and scolds herself, makes excuses for David, and gently rebukes him. Once she addresses him as "Henry" and is shocked.

In the morning, she's frenetically active, doing all the jobs that need doing, one after another, refusing to look at the phone, knowing it won't ring, and listening, listening for it as she swoops from task to task.

At last it's late enough to get ready.

A beautiful meal. Avocados, steaks ready-peppered, and brandy at hand, so they can appear on the table in moments, a triumph of coordination, salad, cheese. There's white wine keeping cold and red wine keeping warm, port, and, for later, a half bottle of champagne upstairs in an ice bucket. A second run of the Friday of the world. Don't miss it, all-star cast, action-packed, they don't make them like that anymore.

Hannah prepares herself with the same care and takes two aspirins instead of tucking her hot-water bottle into her belt. She wears the satin negligee. Finally, with everything the way it ought to be, she takes her place at the window to watch for him. She hopes, she tells herself politely, nice woman, that the interview went well yesterday. Three incarnations indeed. She wouldn't wish that on her worst enemy. Once has been literally all she could cope with. The poor soul must be exhausted after doing it three times over. She smiles faintly and jumps when the phone rings.

"Hullo, Hannah. How are you?"

"Waiting. Everything's waiting." She imagines him smiling into the phone from some pub a couple of miles away, teasing.

"Ah. Well . . . I'm still at Cambridge. It's been very useful, very. Look, I'm not going to be able to get away till late . . ."

Disappointment and fear make her shrill.

"Never mind. It doesn't matter how late . . ."

"No, darling. It'll be too late, truly. I've got to get back. Christine's expecting me."

Shame. He's never made use of Christine before. Unworthy.

"But I'm expecting you."

"Sorry, darling. There's no way I can do it. I'll ring you. 'Bye."

He might as well have hit her. It would have been quicker, thinks Hannah, and at least she'd have had a visible injury to tend.

Feeling sick, she pours sauce into the hollows of the avocados, fries and flames the steaks, dresses the salad, lights the candles, opens the wines. It all looks perfect. She walks around the table and admires it from every angle. It really is a triumph. Superb. How clever she is.

Then she blows out the candles, takes each corner of the tablecloth carefully in her hand and gathers the whole thing up in a crunch of glass and china, a squalid oozing of butter and vinaigrette. It's heavy, but she lifts it, ignoring bits of cheese and salad that spill onto the floor, and heaves it out to the kitchen then out to the dustbin and crams it in, pushing it down as if drowning a hated enemy. Then, her mouth ugly and tight, she goes back to the kitchen and picks up the bottles of cold white wine and warm red wine and a glass and goes back to the living room.

She places the bottles on the table and eyes them, summing them up. Yes, she can manage. Sternly, workmanlike, she starts to drink.

Long before the first bottle's empty she's feeling very sick indeed. She even half rises to go and vomit, but forces herself back into the chair and drinks more.

Then it begins to seem funny. She's done it again. Boobed. Believed in fairy tales. Good old Henry. He has the right approach to fairy tales. A load of sick rubbish, lethal. Hannah starts to laugh. She laughs and laughs, dribbling wine down her satin negligee, till the laughter turns to tears and she cries the bitterest tears of her life, sobbing aloud, moaning, wailing, seeking relief from the brutal pain in her chest. Because though she sees that she imposed her fairy tale on David, she truly believed he loved her.

So the evening passes, now laughter, now tears, and the glass refilled every time it's emptied. It gets late, but she can't go to bed. The bottles aren't empty yet and she has set herself a task. Can't go to bed till it's finished. Must finish what you start. Integrity, Edith said. Poor Edith. She'd understand. She's lived this, for years, till she can't stop. Hannah thanks God she won't have to do that.

She looks at her watch. Two o'clock. Only half a bottle of port left now. What if it doesn't last out till daylight? What will she do then to endure the unendurable, because she believes now that the impossible has happened and David has fallen out of love, and she will never sleep again and she's afraid of the dark. She drinks some more, but it's hard to swallow, so she puts the glass down and rests her head for a moment on the arm of her chair. When she looks at her watch again, it's seven o'clock. She doesn't believe that, she knows she didn't sleep. But never mind. It doesn't matter. Nothing matters.

David doesn't phone till the evening, and Hannah is ill and hung over and desperate. He can't really have stopped loving. It's simply not possible. She's misunderstood. She babbles at him.

"David, what's happened? It's as if you'd stopped loving me. Do you love me? Do you?"

"Of course. Come on, Hannah. What on earth gave you that idea?"

"Say it, then. Say it."

"Hannah, you've jumped to conclusions. You're so wrong."

"Then tell me. Say it." Her voice is drowning, gulping sobs make it ugly, her face burns from salt.

"Hannah. Stop this." There's a steel edge to his voice. "I'll ring you later."

And he hangs up.

And now begins for Hannah the unspectacular nightmare. From the outside, the cottage looks the same. It looked the same when it was empty and when it was occupied by lovers. Inside, Hannah loses touch with day and night. She wanders aimlessly around the rooms. She hardly bothers to wash or dress and eats only when she passes through the kitchen and notices a biscuit or a piece of cheese. She drinks until there's nothing left to drink, smokes all the cigarettes, and then does without. Long, long hours slip away unrecorded. Five minutes of the hideous screaming pain of her loss stretch out to the limit of her tolerance.

He lied. He made promises and broke every one. She believed all of it. He promised. Always, he said. How long is always? She meant forever. He meant till he changed his mind. Is that always? He promised. He said he'd never hurt her. Oh God, not urbane sophisticated God, not singing-and-dancing God, oh God, Mother, help me.

Every day or so he phones and she pretends to be alive and human, talking, listening, but every time it's the same: she says, lightly, "I love you," and there's no response, and she starts to cry, to beg, to plead with him. If he would only, just once, say "I love you," everything would be all right. She could manage then. She probes, tries tricks, giggles girlishly, sobs. She's icy-cold, mortally wounded, furiously angry in turn. He is impatiently silent then, she can hear the irritation vibrate in the silence . . . boring, intractable, troublesome woman. He doesn't hang up, but he won't say it. He will not. So why did he? Playing games. Savage. So why does he keep phoning? Why not leave her alone? He wouldn't do this to an injured dog, he'd dispatch it quick and clean, not keep it breathing, to suffer. Is it because he wants to force her to be the one to say "the end" and so free himself from any taint of blame? She resolves never to answer the phone to him, tries not to, fails, and the whole hideous charade repeats itself.

Now Hannah knows about rejection. Now she knows about hurt and lies and betrayal. Her experience is widened beyond recognition. She ought to be grateful, it was what she wanted, wasn't it? Well, she's got it, and she would eliminate every second of the lovers' delight if as well she could not feel the pain. It's physical. It's corroding her mind. She wants to die. She's sure that she won't go to Hell for her sins. Hell is now. God's got to be fair about it. Not all this and eternal damnation too.

She loathes David. Hates him with a poisonous hatred. If only she didn't love him, if only she could wipe out the image of his face above hers, transformed in the act of love, knowing she'll never see it so again, then it might be tolerated. He's gone from her, and she has nothing to hold to. Not even memories. All their time together was based on love, so Hannah believed. Take away the love and everything's gone, none of it ever happened, because it was created out of something that had no substance. The Emperor's New Clothes.

Her situation is totally shaming in her eyes. She's been used, then discarded. Chewed till all the taste had gone and then spat out. Her nose is being coarsely rubbed in the dirt of having been entirely mistaken, of scoring nought out of ten for judgment, of having allowed unrestricted access to her mind and body to a traitor.

It is beyond bearing. So much for experience. That's not what counts. It's knowing how to apply it and there are no crash courses in that. Hannah's failed again. Oh yes, beyond bearing, but to be borne.

At last, despairing, but with the blessed beginnings of anger, she makes herself stop answering the phone. She's too exhausted anyway. Sometimes she lies on the bed. Sometimes she walks around the cottage. It's deathly quiet because the radio only plays unbearable music, every trite lyric too poignant, too cutting to be tolerated, every melody too sad to endure. Over and over, round and round, her mind torments her with whys and hows. Spasms of forgetfulness ease her into fitful sleep and she has to wake with the horror of bereavement renewed.

Then, after days without names have gone by, the idea of ending her intolerable life comes to Hannah, and she's surprised she hasn't thought of it before. Of course. She's surely had enough Hell now to purge her sins. God's making it easy for her, making death her heart's desire. She can go straight to Heaven, not passing Go, where Mrs. Owen will certainly have the satisfaction of saying, "If only you'd been guided by me . . . you haven't had experience . . . ," but then will look after her, stand between her and God, and not let Him chastise her anymore. Mother won't stand any nonsense from God. What comfort there is in the thought of the stern, forgiving face and strong, rough hands.

How to do it though? One minute she wants violence, blood, torn tissues, horrific mess. The next she wants an unknowing slide into tidy oblivion. She considers cutting her wrists, but there's Edith's paintwork to think of. Natural gas isn't toxic. She has no car with kindly lethal exhaust fumes or a windscreen to be hurled through. She can't get pills without attracting attention. Weedkiller? Oh no. She doesn't want to suffer that kind of agony. So what to do? The problem becomes academic and passes patches of time.

The day that Edith arrives, Hannah is engaged in a long conversation with David. He's not there in the flesh. His shade is sitting on one side of the window seat and Hannah on the other. They have sat thus many and many a time in the days and nights since he destroyed her. She's sometimes icily disdainful, reducing him to bleeding strips of meat with the quiet blade of her tongue. Sometimes piteous, drowning in tears, breaking his shame-filled heart with painfully sobbed words. This time she's a model of dignified suffering, her cheeks wet but her head held high and her voice steady though barely audible. She's telling David all his sins against her, going through his iniquities, itemizing dishonored promises, counting lies, but so gently, so genteelly, that he is stricken with remorse and marvels that he has so carelessly tossed away such nobility, yearns to restore their love, and is destroyed because she will no longer trust him.

Edith opens the door with her key and looks, aghast, at the thin, unkempt figure quietly talking to herself by the window.

"Oh my God," she says.

Hannah is instantly embarrassed. She hasn't lost her mind. She knows quite well how she must look and sound, but she is not mad. She's only able to indulge herself in these cathartic tears and recriminations because the solid ground of reason is beginning to bear her weight, and she needs the ghastly, ghostly conversations because she knows the possibility of communication between her and David has ceased to exist. She needs to say her piece, but he would not hear her any longer. She can never hope to be understood or wanted again, but now she can bear to admit that there's nothing novel in her situation. It's a cliché of a situation, sad, but commonplace. It's the only time it's happened to her, but she feels a desolate comfort in knowing it's so ordinary and that her anguish is a carbon copy of a million others. But it is private. No one should see it. It's like being stripped in public to have one's grief so exposed.

"Hullo, Edith," she says almost normally.

Edith looks nice. The short, wavy hair suits her, softens the angles of her face. The color is less aggressive too, and she wears a lightweight camel coat that eases the excesses of her figure. She doesn't look younger. Whereas before she had no age, now she has, and it's much more becoming.

"Hannah, what on earth are you doing? Henry and I have phoned and phoned and you didn't answer so I've come to see what's happening. Are you all right?"

She sits where the shade of David sat and examines Hannah's face.

"No, you're not. You look terrible."

She takes in at a glance the deteriorated state of her cottage and makes no comment on it.

Hannah wants to lay her head on Edith's shoulder and cry it all out, but that's not permissible, so she sniffs, wipes her face, and says, "I haven't been awfully well. I'm a bit better now."

Edith raises an eyebrow and lets it go at that. She has her suspicions and they're well founded, but she sees no advantage to anyone in voicing them. Instead, she hurries to the shop and buys tins of soup and insists on Hannah's drinking some.

"You've been reading a lot by the look of things," she remarks.

"Yes. I've learned quite a lot."

"That I believe."

"Don't ask me, Edith."

"I wasn't going to." Edith knows when it's kinder to wonder than to ask. "It's time for you to leave here, wouldn't you agree?"

Hannah's alarmed at the thought. It's her last, tenuous link with her Glittering Prize. But it's only an emotional, imaginary link after all. David won't come here anymore. But if she goes home, she'll have to pretend nothing ever happened to her, see David socially from time to time, and pretend, pretend. She'll have to learn him all over again as just a man in the social circle. It will be too much. But she can't stay here. She'll have to go.

"How's Henry?" she asks, not answering Edith's question.

"Very, very worried." Edith's reproving. "You could have phoned, you know. It's been extremely difficult for him to allow you your own way against all his inclinations."

Hannah recognizes that Edith hasn't changed her position, but is merely pointing out that Hannah has been greedier than she needed to be.

"Yes. Poor Henry. He's very good."

Very good. He's let Hannah do it her way, and her way has given her what she wanted and mercilessly shown her that she was much better off without it. He knew that. Mrs. Owen knew. Hannah cried for the moon, the beautiful silver romantic moon, without being willing to understand that the dark side comes as part of the deal. It has caused her to suffer, and Henry would have liked to spare her suffering. He's fended off suffering from all his dependents, always, too much, so that they didn't learn how to manage it, but his motives were unimpeachable.

Is there a way she can thank him, acknowledge his goodness?

Edith tidies up, leaving Hannah by the window to think. And she thinks she's been too selfish. She still wants David.

Though he killed her life, it was she who put the weapon in his hands and she acknowledges that. She loves him unalterably and the loss of him is irreparable, but even if he came now, this minute, and fell on his knees and cried, "I love you, Hannah," she knows with bleak certainty she could never believe him again, and that extinguishes all hope.

She's made another wreckage. She might try to absolve herself by repeating all her old excuses, but it's too late and they no longer carry weight.

What can be salvaged? What reparation can be made?

An honorable surrender, a dignified withdrawal from the field, and an ungrudging performance of penance. There's only one positive, good action left to her, one tribute she can secretly pay to Henry.

"I'll come home with you, Edith, shall I? Henry said I could, any time."

Edith nods approval.

"Let him take charge now. It will make him feel better."

And so she goes home to give Henry back his duty and let him honor his contract.

Twenty

Such a beautiful sunny day. Roses everywhere. The sky is like a Wedgwood plate. How can they cut the grass so short without tearing it, and trim the edges so clean?

Incongruous in black amid such festive color, the Jackson party emerges from the crematorium chapel.

They hang about, not sure what to do next. No one speaks. The vicar has said it all anyway.

"An example to us all of uncomplaining courage. Going about her duties from day to day without complaint. A Good Woman."

Poor Hannah. Poor, poor Hannah.

The big black cars wait, drivers carefully hiding their stubbed-out cigarettes in their pockets so that no disrespectful butts are left to desecrate the smooth gravel.

"What a dreadful smell of burning," Janet suddenly shrills and then blushes to match the roses. George, expressionless, moves away from her. Edith smiles and goes to stand supportively beside her. Cyril's mouth twitches. Henry doesn't hear.

He nods distractedly as people come and take solemn leave of him. His sons are anxious to be away, but dutifully wait behind him, accepting condolences and good-byes as the group breaks up and the cars start to drive away.

"Marvelous roses," George mutters.

"Absolutely marvelous," Henry's mother pipes, looking small and frail and anxious, as if she's afraid someone may keep her here to save themselves another journey before long.

"I expect," Janet disastrously digs herself deeper in, "I expect they put something on the soil."

This time Cyril catches Edith's eye and has to turn away.

Edith is in charge. She looks nice in black. A nice, competent, middle-aged woman. The year that's passed has done her good, and Cyril. They've had a chance to examine the options open to them.

David and Christine are talking to Henry. He makes an effort to pay attention.

"Thank you, thank you," he says conventionally. "Everyone's been very kind."

Then he registers that it's David.

"Thanks, David," he says. "It was good of you to get her interested in things. Took her out of herself. She was a different woman after doing that article with you last year. Not different . . . she was the way she used to be when we were first married. So contented with her home and all the little things . . ."

David's expression doesn't change.

"I didn't know she was ill then," he says. "I wouldn't have asked . . ."

"She didn't want concessions," Henry assures him kindly. "She enjoyed being involved. Did her good."

David has no answer. Christine takes his arm and holds out her hand to Henry.

"Good-bye, Henry. We'll see you soon."

"Yes. Good-bye." Henry doesn't care if they stay or go as long as they leave him alone.

Edith organizes Mrs. Jackson into a car with her grandsons, sees Janet and George off, separate in the same car, waves a good-bye to Christine and David.

"Christine's turn again?" Cyril speculates on the strength of a year's acquaintance.

"For the moment, I think. Until next time."

Cyril puts an arm around Edith's shoulder. She doesn't need to look at him to know she's won, but she doesn't see it as a victory. She doesn't want a victory any longer. Rather a quiet end to an exhausting journey. Not the destination she'd set out for, but it will have to do because there's no time or energy for more miles. She's glad they're not young anymore and carrying weapons. Hannah, if she did nothing else, succeeded in disarming them. Perhaps time on its own could have done it, but the chances are against it. Cyril is glad to be safe home, wearing a twenty-two-carat chain to hold him back, because he finds he's afraid of challenging Dragons now. Dragons are getting bigger and younger every year. Let David do the Dragon-killing. It's too risky and the rewards don't seem as rewarding as they used to.

In the car, going home, Edith sits between Henry and Cyril.

"Well, Henry," she says, "it's over. You did all you could."

"Yes, I did, didn't I?" He wants confirmation. "What could I have done differently?"

"Nothing, dear. You looked after her wonderfully well."

"Going to sell the house and move away?" Cyril brashly asks.

Henry doesn't mind. He's looking out of the window.

"No," he answers at length. "No, I'm not. I'll just carry on as usual. I've got Mother to take care of, and I've got my work and my book."

"There's no need to decide anything just yet," Edith says. "Rest for a while. It's been a hard year for you. You've nothing to blame yourself for. You tried to give Hannah all she wanted and she was really grateful. She told me how much she loved and admired you for it."

"Did she?" He livens up. "Did she say that?"

"Yes, Henry. She did. She said you were very good to her."

He shrinks again.

"I did try. I honestly tried, and she was so sweet and quiet and pretty. And so brave at the end. But the truth is, Edith, I still don't understand. Off and on last year, in all that fuss, I sometimes felt I could see her point, but now she's gone, I don't understand what the hell she was going on about."

Everyone knows goats don't kill wolves. Not even in fairy tales.

186